Body
on the Church
Steps

By

Paul J. Stam

Stiletto Books
Published by Indigo Sea Press
Winston-Salem

Stiletto Books
Indigo Sea Press
302 Ricks Drive
Winston-Salem, NC 27103

First Stiletto Books edition published
December, 2015
Stiletto Books, Moon Sailor, and all production design are trademarks of Indigo Sea Press, used under license.

For information regarding bulk purchases of this book, digital purchase and special discounts, please contact the publisher at indigoseapress.com

Cover design by Stacy Castanedo
Cover Art by Norm Graffam, Windward Community College, Hawaii

Manufactured in the United States of America
ISBN 978-1-63066-373-5

Dedication

This book is dedicated to all those who read this book when they should be doing something earthshaking—-there are so few earth-shakers around anymore.

CHAPTER ONE

She was young, exceptionally beautiful, and except for her sheer lace panties, completely naked and very dead. She lay at the top of the steps that led up to the front of the church. If you stood in just the right place you could see two of her, her real self and her reflection in the large, plate-glass, front doors to the church. Her head was turned to hang over the top step with her long, blond hair cascading down over the next two steps. Her right arm lay stretched out on the second step and her left arm was thrown back over her head. She looked as though she had been arranged to have a picture taken for an art calendar or some magazine. It was hard to believe that someone so young and beautiful was dead. But then it was also hard to imagine anyone alive would be lying naked on the church steps.

In the early morning light it was too perfect a picture to contain death. Her open eyes looked up to the clear blue of the Hawaiian sky, which matched the color of her eyes. The white, billowing clouds drifted over the tops of the Ko`olau range just as they were supposed to. Hawaiian tradition said that if ever there were no clouds over those mountains the island would sink into the sea.

Between the church and the office building, was a large mango tree. It always produced a great abundance of fruit, but the fruit was small and stringy and not worth bothering with. Consequently the fruit dropped to the ground staining the sidewalks; attracting flies, and creating a lumpy and slippery hazard for those trying to climb the steps.

Several of the mangoes had bounced and rolled to within a few feet of the dead woman's left hand. If you had looked down from God's vantage point it would have looked as though the woman had scattered the fallen fruit with the hand flung back over her head like a sower scattering seed.

Pastor Douglas Bautista discovered her at 6:10 when he arrived at the church. A few others, driving by in the morning traffic who glanced that direction at exactly the right moment saw the body before he did. The glimpse was so fleeting the only thing they could think of was that someone was playing a practical joke on the church

1

by laying a mannequin on the church steps.

The church custodian, Radford Lee, had also seen the body. He had unlocked the side doors to the church at five-thirty for those who might stop in for prayer on their way to work. After unlocking the side doors he walked through the church to the foyer and wondered why the foyer lights and the outdoor, front floodlights were not on. He distinctly remembered turning them on the evening before. He was about to unlock the front door when looking through the glass doors he saw the woman. He was startled at first and stood for a while behind the glass doors, running a hand nervously through his wavy brown hair. He stood just staring at her and wondering what he should do. Under the circumstances he thought it best not to unlock the front door. He thought she was dead, but he wasn't absolutely sure. He didn't quite know how to handle a naked woman on the church steps. If she was alive and drunk, he thought it best not to be seen handling her.

He had learned, soon after he started working at the church, that it was a lot simpler not to get involved in the problems people brought with them to the church. The woman did not appear sick or hurt, therefore he concluded that she must be dead, or drunk, or pulling a stunt to get attention. From where he stood he couldn't tell for certain if she was breathing or not. Maybe she was protesting something. His logical conclusion was that if she were dead there was nothing he could do for her, and if it was a publicity stunt he didn't want to get caught up in it.

Radford walked back into the church and left by the side door. He used the back entrance to the classroom building, and after turning of the alarm walked through to the church offices. He went about emptying the wastebaskets. From time to time he would set down the plastic bag full of waste paper and walk to the window. He would part the blinds a little, and look out at her. Each time he looked out at her he became more certain that she was dead and that became increasingly more frightening. It was very unlikely that anyone would get naked to go and die on church steps of natural causes. He was certain therefore that she had been murdered and that he had made the right decision in not discovering a murder victim.

Although Radford had actually seen the body first, Pastor Bautista took credit for it. He approached from the parking lot behind the buildings. He was a short, stocky Filipino with straight, black hair and black eyes. He was wearing a Greek fisherman's cap and an Aloha shirt of red and yellow Hibiscus flowers. He walked with a swagger as he made his way through the yard glancing to the left and the right looking for something about which he could be righteously angry. He noted that the leaves and fallen fruit had not been raked up from under the mango tree in the schoolyard. Children attending the pre-school would start arriving in half an hour, and the leaves and fruit were supposed to be cleaned up by then. Radford was supposed to rake up the fallen fruit first thing in the morning and it pleased Bautista that it had not yet been done it. It would give him something about which to scold Radford.

Bautista was just about to start up the mango splattered steps to the office when he looked the other direction and saw the body. He went over to it and walked completely around it once having to go down a few steps and then up again to get around it. From the way her open eyes stared out at the world he knew she was dead, but still he knelt down and put his fingers on her wrist feeling for a pulse. That close to her he could see a lone ant going to the right, then to the left, sometimes back the way it had come as it made its investigative way up the ascent of her breast toward the nipple.

He stood up, and swaggered up the steps, and into the office. He found Radford vacuuming the reception area. "Go get me a sheet, Radford."

"What?" Radford asked turning off the vacuum.

"Get me a sheet."

"A sheet? What kind of sheet? Do you mean a drop cloth?"

"A sheet, Radford. Any kind of sheet. A sheet to cover the body."

"What body, Pastor Doug?" Radford said pretending complete ignorance.

Pastor Bautista looked at him for a moment and then said, "There is a body of a dead woman on our front steps. Get me a sheet to cover her."

"There is? Oh, my goodness! Where did it come from?" he said hoping he had accurately conveyed shock and disbelief. "We don't have any sheets that I know of."

"Find something. Go to the baptismal room and get me one of the baptismal robes. One that isn't assigned to anyone."

"Yes, Sir," Radford said leaving and Pastor Bautista sat down in the receptionist chair and in his excitement dialed 119. He leaned back in the chair and looked at the ceiling wondering why it didn't ring.

A voice came on which said, "If you wish to make a call, please

3

hang up and dial again."

He hung up and dialed 119 again, and then suddenly realized his mistake, and quickly hung up and dialed 911, and got a response.

By the time Radford returned with the baptismal robe, and Bautista finished explaining everything to the police, and they went out to cover the body, news trucks from three television stations were already there taking pictures of the body. Bautista wondered how they could have gotten there so quickly. He had just called the police. The cameramen were being genuinely ingenious at finding ways to get a picture that had both the body and the name of the church in it. He roughly pushed the cameramen aside as he went over and very piously laid the baptismal robe over the body. When he was through she was demurely covered with only her head, her feet and her arms exposed to the prying eyes of the cameras.

When he straightened up the cameras were on him and three reporters held their microphones in front of him. "Would you tell us your name, Sir?" one of the reporters asked.

He took the fisherman's cap off his head and turned slightly so as to give the cameras a good three-quarters shot of his best side. "I'm the Reverend Douglas Bautista. I'm the Senior Associate Pastor here at First Aloha Christian Tabernacle."

"Did you discover the body?"

"Yes, I think so. At least no one reported it to the police before I did."

"Do you know the young lady? Is she a member of your church?"

"No, I do not know her, and she is not a member of the church."

"Did she attend this church?"

"She may have from time to time. But we have more than a thousand in attendance every Sunday. There are a lot of people that might drop in for a service that we never get to know personally. I don't recognize her. I don't remember ever having seen her before in my life. I don't think she is on our steps because she attended here."

"Then why do you think her body is here?"

"I have no idea."

In the distance they could hear the sirens of a police car trying to get through the morning traffic.

"Now I think, gentlemen, that we should save any more questions you might have until the police get here."

The reporters kept trying to ask him questions and he kept putting them off. It made him feel important to have them all trying

4

to get a question answered, and it made him feel even more important to not answer their questions.

Three squad cars, with blue lights flashing, arrived almost simultaneously congesting the traffic even more than the TV trucks had. Soon after that there was an ambulance, and then two more police cars till the one-way traffic on the two-lane road in front of the church was reduced to one lane. Drivers going by slowed things even more by trying to see what was happening, and residents from the nearby high-rises started gathering on their lanais looking down wondering what the fuss was all about. Others came out of their buildings and talked excitedly into their cell phones telling friends and family what they were seeing.

The police moved in quickly stringing up yellow ribbons that said, CRIME SCENE - DO NOT CROSS. A detective started questioning Bautista and he told them what he told the reporters.

"Are you the one that covered the body?" The detective asked.

"Yes."

"You shouldn't have done that, you know. That was disturbing the evidence."

"I couldn't just leave her there for everyone to see. This is, after all, a church."

The detective looked at him as if to say, 'so what?' and asked. "Did you touch the body at all?"

"Just to take her pulse."

"Oh? And just where was that: at her wrist, her neck, her stomach? Just where did you touch her?" he asked sneering.

"I resent the implication of that question."

"Just answer the question."

"Her wrist."

"And then what did you do?"

"I went into the office and told the janitor to go get the robe. Then I called the police."

"Did you also call the TV people?"

"No. The police were the only people I called. I'm sure you have a recording of my call. By the time I finished explaining everything to you people the janitor had come back with the robe and we came out and covered her."

Radford told the police that he had not seen the woman until he came out with Pastor Bautista to cover the body. He too did not remember ever having seen her at the church before. He was certain he had turned on the floodlights at the front of the church and the

5

lights in the foyer the evening before. With the lights on it would have been hard for anyone to walk up the steps and not be seen. With them off the area of the steps would have been almost completely dark.

"Could anyone have turned them off after you turned them on?" the detective asked.

"Lots of people have keys. Anyone could have gone in and turned off the lights."

"Who, for example has keys to the church?"

"Lots of people. All the pastors, all ministry leaders, all of the schoolteachers, all have keys because they all have to get into the sanctuary. And there might be people that have keys that we don't know about."

"How's that?"

Radford shrugged his shoulders and ran a hand through his wavy brown hair pushing it back from his face. "They loan a key out and forget who they loaned it to."

"How many such missing keys do you think there are?"

"I have no idea."

"Is the sanctuary locked most of the time?"

"No. It's always opened during the day. People come into pray and there is something scheduled in there almost every day."

The crowd of spectators grew as parents who came to drop their children off at the school stuck around to find out what was happening contributing to the traffic jam in front of the church.

"Now you're sure you turned the lights on before you went home last night."

"Yes. I'm sure. Someone might have turned them off thinking they shouldn't be on during the day."

"What time did you turn them on?"

"Five. Five fifteen. It was still light out."

"That's pretty early to be turning lights on isn't it?"

"I had a class at U.H. I leave a little earlier than usual on Mondays. That's why I have to come in early on Tuesdays to clean up the offices."

"But when you left the church was locked and the lights were on?"

"Yes. I think so."

"What do you mean you think so?"

"Well, I don't really check all the doors because on Mondays Momi does that for me."

6

"Was she still here when you left?"

"Oh, yes. There were lots of people here. There are pre-school people who are waiting for parents to come a pick up their kids. And the secretaries are all here until five-thirty every day. I don't think there were any pastors here because Monday is their day off."

"Well, I guess that's all for right now, but we may have some more questions later."

The staff was continuing to arrive. Each, in one way or another learned what had happened, and the detectives informed each that they would all be questioned. Pastor Bell arrived and very graciously, but firmly told the detectives that the staff morning devotions were at eight-thirty and everyone was required to be there. He invited the detectives to join them, but the detectives declined saying that they would be back after nine to talk to the staff. They assured everyone that it was just routine, but since the body had been found on the church steps they had to talk to everyone employed by the church.

"I understand," Pastor Bell said, and went into his office until it was time for devotions.

Betty Clipper burst into the reception area at 8:25 screaming, "Is it true?—Was there really a dead girl on our steps?—Oh, My God. I can't believe it.—What are we going to do?—Was it anyone we knew?—Oh, Dear Jesus, this is terrible."

She was a large woman, just over six feet tall, and weighing almost two hundred pounds. She had the title of Music Minister, and was in charge of all the musical groups in the church. She loved to sing solos, which she did fairly well and was a very acceptable pianist. Unfortunately she was built more like a man than a woman, and was not graceful in any way.

"I can't believe it. I'm shaking so much I can hardly stand," she said dropping her bulk into the closest chair.

"The reason you're shaking, Betty, is because your legs are too spindly to hold up all the weight of your body," Doug said looking down on her. His dark eyes gleamed with hatred because she was a haole, a woman, and when standing taller than he was.

She started to cry. "Can't you see this is a hard enough time for me, Doug, without your picking on me. This thing really has me scared."

"Oh, stop crying, Betty. You have nothing to be afraid of. No one would want to kill you or do anything else to you for that matter," Doug answered.

7

Pastor Bell walked in just after that and Doug suddenly became seriously pious.

"Betty. Betty. What's wrong? Nobody's going to hurt you. We all love you," Pastor Bell said walking toward her.

Betty stood up and cried that much louder going over to him like a child that needed to be comforted. He put an arm around her and let her cry on his shoulder.

"It's all right, Betty. You go ahead and cry if you want to. This thing has all of us a little upset."

He comforted her until the sound portion of her crying was on mute, and then sent her back to her chair sniffling, and wiping at her tears with a soggy tissue.

Pastor Bell sat down then and started the devotion by singing a chorus, and the others joined in. But the singing was not very sincere and when it came time for the devotional, Don Bjork, who was to do the Scripture reading and bring the devotional message that morning, spoke about how the events of the morning should make them aware of just how uncertain life was, and they should all be living righteously.

The prayers were mostly that the family of the dead girl would know the comfort of the Holy Spirit. None of them knew who the girl was, or who her family was, but it was a safe thing to pray. No one prayed that the police would quickly find the killer of the woman, which surprised Jim Sloan, who, although he was one of the pastors, did not really believe in prayer.

By the time devotions were over the police were through with the front steps of the church, and the crowd of spectators separated as the coroner took the body away. The TV cameras tried to focus on the stretcher as it moved from the steps to the coroner's van. The police started spreading out around the church, looking behind the shrubbery while the detectives went into the church office building to talk to the staff.

CHAPTER TWO

The flight from San Francisco made its turn over Barbers Point and started its final approach to Honolulu International Airport. Those not sitting by the windows were straining to see past those who had window seats hoping for their first glimpse of Paradise. In her first-class, aisle seat, Jacqueline Marqueoff was not interested, or particularly excited, about arriving in Hawaii even though it was her first trip. On the visitor's information form she had put her reason for coming to Hawaii as business, but it wasn't a pleasant business. In her purse she had a letter that she had read so many times she had it memorized.

Dear Jackie,

I think I've found him, and I think he knows who I am, and why I'm here. I know you said we were not to put anything in writing, but I tried calling you several times, and got a message that your number was no longer in service. I am desperate. I think he is trying to kill me. Please call me!!!

Susan.

Jackie felt guilty that she hadn't been able to get hold of her sister Susan who had returned to Honolulu to try and find out who had killed their sister Cynthia. After Cynthia's body had been taken back to San Francisco for burial, Susan had returned to Hawaii to see if she could find out how Cynthia had really died. The Honolulu police claimed that Cynthia had died of a drug overdose, but there was something totally wrong with that because Cindy was a health freak who didn't use drugs.

The breakdown in communication between Jackie and Susan happened when Jackie moved. Jackie had stopped service at the old landline number before service at the new number started. It had been a mix-up with the phone company that had her without landline service for a few days. At the same time, in the confusion of moving, she had misplaced her cell phone. She bought a new cell and when her landline service resumed she had tried calling Susan and when she got no answer was not particularly concerned until she got the letter.

After she got the letter she tried calling every hour for more than a day, and then had decided to jump a plane, and contact Susan in person. She kept telling herself that she would find Susan all right, that Susan's letter was just over reacting, that Susan had just gone off somewhere for a few days. When Susan returned Jackie would be furious with her, but right now Jackie was more concerned than angry.

Being from San Francisco the heat and humidity of Paradise was somewhat of a shock to Jacqueline when she stepped out of the air-conditioned arrival area. The wind whipped through the open concourse tugging at her skirt and the lapels of her suit jacket. In the open area between the shops in the main terminal area the wind had already disarranged the synthetic red and silver garlands on the artificial Christmas tree which had been put up just the week before. The Christmas decorations in the shop windows and concourses of the airport seemed incorrect surrounded by the warmth and the sound of rustling palm fronds.

At the baggage area she tried again to call Susan while waiting for the baggage to arrive. She let the phone ring eleven times, and then turned off her cell irritated and upset. When she turned back to the carousel the people were packed so tightly around it trying to get their baggage that she stood to one side looking about for a sky-cap while waiting for the crowd to thin out.

She knew that she looked out of place. She was the only woman there in a suit, high heels and nylons. She was a tall woman with thick, naturally wavy, light brown, almost blond hair and blue eyes that usually had a smile about them, Right now the smile had been driven undercover by severe worry. She would not have been considered a ravenous beauty but she was attractive in a poised, dignified, commanding way that made people; both men and women, turn to look at her as she passed.

She stood patiently because she had the talent, which is rare in both men and women, to know what was, and what was not, really important. Susan's letter was important. Not being able to get a hold of Susan was important. Having to wait for luggage was not important. An even greater rare gift was the ability not to transfer her sense of the urgency for the important to the unimportant. Consequently, she could wait perfectly calmly for her luggage to arrive without feeling about it the urgency she felt to find Susan.

The apartment, which had been Cynthia's before she died, and most recently used by Susan, was on the top floor of a three-story low-rise. Walking up the two flights of stairs with a suitcase in each hand she wished she had brought fewer clothes, and had not worn

10

high heels and stockings. At the top of the stairs she set the suitcases down, and rested for a moment.

Apartment 305 was at the far end, but she could at least pull her suitcases along on their wheels. They made a terrible noise rolling along the cement walkway. At the apartment next to Cynthia's, a man wearing surfer shorts came to his screen door to watch her walk by. He smiled at her and she thought that if she didn't find Susan right away he would be one place to start asking questions. There was a stair way at each end of the building, but the one at her end was a gated fire escape through which you could leave but not enter, consequently everything that went to, or came from, the end apartment would have had to go by his door. He impressed her as the curious kind that checked on everything that went by his door.

Jacqueline let herself in. Jackie and Susan both had a set of keys to their sister Cynthia's apartment. Cynthia had sent them each a set when she had found the apartment. Her note had said, "You might as well each have these. Just in case you decide to come over and I'm not at the apartment when you arrive."

Jackie pulled the suitcases in behind her, leaving them by the door, dropping her carry-on next to them and walked through the combination living-dining room to the screen door to the lanai. There was a glass top table with two metal chairs on the lanai. The screen door was locked but the sliding glass door was open as were all the louvered windows. Susan had obviously not intended to be gone for a long time.

The kitchen was an alcove at the lanai end of the main room. She looked in the refrigerator and there was the reasonable amount of food for someone living alone. None of it was spoiled, or moldy, which meant that Susan had not been gone that long.

Next to the kitchen area was a bathroom about the size of the kitchen, and next to that was the bedroom. She stepped into the small bedroom, and looked around quickly. There was a twin bed, a large dresser with an assortment of bottles, hand mirrors, and brushes on the top. In a corner at the foot of the bed was a television set on a stand. Next to the bed there was another stand with a clock, some books, and a telephone. There were no messages on the phone. She noticed that even the louvers of the ceiling-high windows in the bedroom were open.

She went back into the living room, and sat down on the wicker couch, and looked around. There was another chair that matched the couch, a coffee table and on the opposite wall a bookshelf with

11

books. In one corner there was an exercise machine. It wasn't much of an apartment really. There was nothing wrong with it, but it was just one room that reached from the front door to the lanai and off of it were the bedroom, the bath and the kitchen.

Jacqueline Marqueoff was ten years old when her cousins, Susan and Cynthia Harcourt, came to live with them. Susan and Cynthia's parents were killed in an auto accident and the girls had gone to live with their uncle and aunt. The three girls had grown up like sisters, closer than sisters. A year ago Susan and Cynthia had taken a vacation trip to Hawaii. When the vacation was supposed to be over Cynthia told Susan that she was going to stay on, and got the apartment, and a job as a nude dancer. That was a year ago, and all during that time all they heard from Cindy was how much she was loving Hawaii. Then six weeks ago they had gotten a call from the police that Cynthia had been found dead of an overdose.

Susan had flown to Honolulu to claim the body and accompany it back to San Francisco. When she got to Honolulu Susan had learned that they had found Cynthia in a sleazy hotel in downtown Honolulu. The police had been very nonchalant about it, just another nude dancer that had overdosed. Cynthia may have been a nude dancer, but Jackie and Susan both knew she was also a health nut. She was careful about her diet, did not smoke or drink, and most certainly didn't use drugs.

When Cynthia first told her sisters that she was dancing in clubs they had not been shocked. Jacqueline's reaction had been more one of shrugging her shoulders and thinking, "Well, that's Cindy for you." If she was a nude dancer it was because she was proud of her beautiful body, liked to dance, and saw her dancing as getting paid for doing aerobic exercises. For both Jackie and Susan there was something very wrong about the way Cynthia had died, and the police were not doing anything about it.

After the funeral in San Francisco, Susan had returned to Honolulu. She wanted to find out what she could about her sister's death, and then collect Cynthia's things, get rid of the furniture, and close the apartment. Susan had called Jackie every day, until there had been the mix-up with the telephones when Jackie moved. Sitting there in Cynthia's apartment Jackie was overcome with emotion. Not only was there the grief of Cynthia's death, but also the fear of not knowing where Susan was.

Surrounded by Cindy's things she permitted herself to cry for only a few minutes and then dried her tears. She undressed and in only her bra and panties washed her face and started to unpack. With each article of clothing that she tried to fit into the already crowded closet she was reminded of both her sisters. She would see something of Cynthia's, and the tears would come to her eyes again. Then she would see something of Susan's hanging next to it, and she would become concerned. When she finished putting her things away she got dressed in blouse and shorts.

She fixed herself a cup of tea, and took it out to the lanai. It was pleasant out there. It was the middle of the afternoon, and the lanai was in the shade. She thought that it probably got the morning sun, which was the way Cynthia would have wanted it. A cooling breeze was blowing through the apartment from the front door to where she was sitting. Over the roofs of the buildings below her she could see to the high-rise hotels and condominiums of Waikiki and beyond them the ocean.

She had finished her tea, and was just sitting there when the phone rang. She went into the bedroom to answer it, but before she could get there she heard Cindy's voice saying, "This is 523-8820. We can't take your call right now but if you leave your name and number we will call you back."

The sound of Cindy's voice brought tears to her eyes. Susan had not bothered to change message. There was no incoming message, just an ominous silence before the click of whoever was calling hung up.

She sat down on the bed and looked around the room, looking for anything that might tell her where Susan was. In the drawer of the bedside table she found an address book that had obviously been Cynthia's. The book contained mostly girl's names and telephone numbers with an occasional address. There were sheets from a yellow pad struck in the book with Susan's handwriting. A lot of the names and numbers on Susan's yellow sheets were the same as those in Cynthia's book. She tried to find something on the yellow sheets that would tell her where Susan had gone, but didn't find anything. She started going through every book in the bookcase, holding each by the binding and shaking it for any scrap of paper to fall out, and thought as she did it that Susan had probably already done that.

She sat down on the bed with the list of Susan's phone numbers in front of her, and was about to start making calls when she decided to check the mailbox. The man in the apartment next door came to his door as she approached, and she smiled at him as she passed. There was nothing in the mailbox except catalogues addressed to Cynthia Harcourt or Occupant.

The neighbor was waiting for her as she returned. "How'z it?" he said as she approached.

He was muscular and broad shouldered with long wavy black hair that was pulled back away from his face into a ponytail. He had the stance of a wrestler with large, strong looking hands. If he had been a little taller he would have been very close to the kind of Hawaiian man the Tourist Bureau would want pictured on its brochures.

"Hello," she said.

"You move in, or what?" he eyed her suspiciously.

"Just for a little while. Did you know the girl that lived there before me?"

"Like 'fore you last week, or 'fore dat?

"Last week."

"I seen her, I not know her. She not here long. She gone now? You moving in, or what?" he asked again eyeing her distrustfully.

"And what about the girl before her? Cynthia?" Jackie asked ignoring his questions.

"Cindy? Know her real good. She good friend with my seestah. Sometimes we talk story, and like that. You know her, or what?"

"I was a friend of hers."

"You a dancer too? She one terrific dancer. The max," he said smiling proudly.

"No, just a friend."

"Good friend?" he asked prying.

"Yes."

"Too bad how she die. You wanna come in?" He was suddenly very serious and solicitous.

"No, thank you. I really can't stop," she said starting to leave, and then turned back, and said, "How did she die?"

"Drugs. Bad, man. Bad," he said shaking his head. "It bad pilakia all ovah."

"Pilakia?" she asked thinking it was some kind of drug.

"Trouble. Bad trouble. Drugs."

"That's what the police told us, but how do you know it was drugs?"

"Police not ask where she work. Cops say she die from overdose. Da dancers say she not use drugs, but cops no believe dem."

"Where did she work?"

"Everywhere. Krazy Kat, Lollipop, Club Yu-Me, Butterfly. All over. Everywhere."

14

"For someone that you say was so good she didn't stay with one club very long."

"They not jus work da one club. Every night they do da show one place then go next club, do show there, go next place. She the best, man. She so good plenty men follow her she go club to club."

"I see. Well, it was nice meeting you. Maybe I'll see you again sometime," she said turning to leave.

"My name Kimo. I good friend with Cindy. Friend. Dat's all. We all time talk story. All morning sometime we talk story. I be friend with you too. Anybody give you pilakia, you call Kimo," He said poking his bare chest with his thumb. "My seestah and me, we good friend with Cindy."

"Thank you, Kimo. My name's Jackie," she said starting toward her apartment and then again turned back just remembering, and asked, "Is your sister's name, Marcella? Does she own a Hawaiian supply shop?"

"We own."

"Cindy talked about Marcella. She said Marcella was her friend, but I didn't know she was a next-door neighbor. Cindy was my sister."

"Awe, sorry. Real sorry bout Cindy."

"Maybe your sister and I can talk later." She felt herself on the verge of tears, and said quickly, "I've got to go now," and headed for the apartment.

She sat down on the bed until she had composed herself, and then spread out the papers making notations of the names, and numbers that were in both Cynthia's book, and on Susan's sheets of yellow note paper. She really didn't feel up to making phone calls right away. When she started making calls she wanted to be fully alert so she could catch any hesitations, or voice inflections that might tell her something the person was not saying. It was only five in the evening, but it was two hours later by San Francisco time, and her mind and body was suffering from jet lag. She leaned back on the bed, and taking the remote from the nightstand turned on the television to catch the evening news.

The sound came on with the words before the picture came on: "The nude body of a dead woman is found on the steps of a local church by one of its pastors."—"The City Council opposes the State on the latest proposal for affordable housing."—"A snow storm blankets the northeast Mainland."—"These stories and much more when the news continues in just two minutes. Stay with us."

She almost fell asleep during the commercials that preceded the news, but opened her eyes when the anchorman said, "The body of a dead woman was found early this morning on the steps of the First Aloha Christian Tabernacle. The woman was naked, and was found by one of the pastors. Early indications are that the woman was poisoned. For more on the story we go now John Delegardo who was at the scene."

The camera opened on the field reporter, and then went to the name of the church, and finally to the woman lying on the steps. The screen showed the woman with some kind of maroon gown over her. Jacqueline sat upright on the bed leaning toward the TV set. There was no question that the woman on the steps was Susan. Jackie was both shocked and angry. It was insensitive of the television people to show that kind of picture. The picture of Susan lying there was insensitive, startling, unbelievable, and devastating.

She was about to turn the set off not knowing who to call first, the police, or the TV station when the camera moved to a young man taking off a Greek fisherman's cap, and saying, "I'm the Reverend Douglas Bautista. I'm the Senior Associate Pastor here at the Aloha Christian Tabernacle."

She started shuffling through the yellow papers looking for the name. She knew she had seen it. She wished she had put the names in alphabetical order. She found it finally in the middle of a sheet of yellow paper. There was an X next to it, which meant that it had also been in Cynthia's book. She held the piece of paper with his name and its X, and started shaking with anger as he told the reporter that he didn't know Susan, had never seen her before. *How could he say that? Cynthia and Susan both had his name, and phone number.*

The program went back to the studio, and a picture of Susan, just her face this time, appeared in a box above the anchor's shoulder. "The police have not been able to identify the victim, and there are no suspects at this time. If you have any information as to the identity of this woman you are asked to call 911 or 943-3355 and ask for Detective Kunayoshi."

The telephone numbers, and the name, came on the bottom of the screen and she wrote them down, and then started to cry clutching the yellow piece of paper with Bautista's name on it to her chest.

Through her sobbing, and gasping for air, she began to realize the pounding she heard was someone knocking on her door. "Go away!" she shouted.

"Eh! Jackie, what's the matter fo you? It's Kimo. You let me in,

16

OK? I no go way."

She knew somehow that he wouldn't leave, and for some reason it just seemed easier to open the door than to listen to him pounding on it. She went and opened the door just a crack with the chain still on, and stood so he couldn't see her eyes, and said, "Kimo. I appreciate your trying to help, but I just heard some very bad news, and there's nothing you can do right now."

"I see on the news. That girl. She lived here before you. She friend? Family?"

"She was my other sister."

"She Cindy seestah too then?"

"Yes," she said nodding a little.

"Eh! Dat beeg bummah," he said, "My seestah home now. You come our place. No good be all by self like dis." He turned, and called over his shoulder. "Eh, Marcella, come heah foe minute, yeah?"

"I don't think so. I'd like to be alone. I'll be all right."

"No good alone. All lone you tink all kine bad tings. Bess be wit people." A young woman wearing a flowered muu-muu walked up, and he said, "She jus heah on da news her seestah make. Da one church side. Das why she make all da cryin."

"Oh, I'm so sorry. I really am. Why don't you come to our apartment for a little while? We don't want to intrude on you, but it isn't good for you to be alone. Is there someone you want us to call to come and stay with you?"

Jackie shook her head.

"Then come be with us for a little while. You don't have to talk if you don't want to, but it's not good for you to be all alone."

"I'm all right. I've got to call the police," she said in a bewildered sort of way.

"No! No! No call da kine," Kimo said shaking his head emphatically. "You get one lepo not knowin' nuttin."

"He's right," Marcella said. "Kunayoshi, or whatever his name is, has gone home for the day, and you'd just get someone that didn't know what they were doing. Besides, you can't do anything for your sister by talking to the police tonight. Wait until morning when you're rested and feeling better. Kimo can drive you to the police station tomorrow if you like. Now why don't you come home with us? Come on," Marcella coaxed.

"OK," Jackie said undoing the chain, and opening the door. She was shaking her head as though she didn't know exactly what she

17

was doing. Marcella put a comforting arm around her as she led her along the walkway to their apartment.

CHAPTER THREE

The morning devotions were over and James Sloan hurried to his office eager to hear what those in the offices around him would have to say. He had not been able to learn anything particularly interesting the day before. There had been too much confusion with people going in and out because of the police questioning everyone.

This morning after devotions Pastor Bell had said, "Doug, could I see you in my office for a minute?"

The way Pastor Bell said it, Sloan knew Pastor Bell was upset about something, and Sloan wanted to get to his office, and hear the conversation between Pastor Bell and Doug from the very beginning. Sloan had always been interested in listening in on other people's conversations.

Jim Sloan was not interested in being a spy, as such, but the challenge and apparatus of spying on other people had always intrigued him. He loved the gadgets in James Bond movies. His parents were pleased that he spent his time reading electronic books, and magazine articles, with such titles as, "Build your own radio" rather than pouring over comic books. When he was in the eighth grade he put together his first little transmitter and receiver. He placed the transmitter in his parents' bedroom, and for a while was able to hear his parents' conversation, and a lot more that he didn't quite understand. He never shared the things he heard with his brothers and sister, but there was definite advantages knowing ahead of time what his parents were thinking of doing. Unfortunately his mother found the transmitter attached to the back of the headboard one day when she was cleaning, and not knowing what it was, threw it out.

Jimmy Sloan had gone to a private, Christian high school. By the time he was a sophomore in high school he had improved his transmitters and receivers, and was able to bug the girls' washroom, which was right next to the photo lab. He, and his best friend Mike, would listen to the girls' conversations while they developed pictures they had taken with their hidden camera. What they heard shocked them sometimes, but they never told anyone else what they heard. But sometimes they would be talking to some girl, and smile secretly knowing things about her she did not know they knew.

One Saturday during a Student-Parents' Clean-up Day he was able to bug the school's outer office. With that he was able to know what kind of trouble other kids in school were in. He also learned that Mr. Flemming was having an affair with both Miss Glenup, one of the English teachers, and Miss Schilling the receptionist. He never told Mike about Mr. Flemming. The thrill of spying to him was knowing things no one else knew. If he told Mike the exclusivity of it would be gone. He also knew that if the church school board ever found out about Flemming, Glenup, and Schilling, they would all be fired. He liked Mr. Flemming and didn't want him fired, but it used to amuse him when Flemming would stand up in front of assembly and start preaching to them. And he couldn't help fantasizing about Miss Glenup. But then, Miss Glenup was a woman many of the boys in high school fantasized, and talked, about.

By the time he was in college He was able to buy good quality bugging devices through mail-order catalogue. In college his interest in history came about as an outgrowth of his spying. It was a desire to know things about heroes that no one else, or at least very few people, knew. His masters' studies was in Church History, and his doctoral thesis was on *The Dark Side of Renaissance Popes.*

Dr. James Sloan was the only one on the staff with an earned doctorate. He never referred to himself as Doctor Sloan, but everyone on the staff, and in the congregation, was aware of it. The fact that he didn't flaunt it, hardly ever mentioned it himself, made it that much more obvious to the congregation, because Pastor Bell always referred to him as Doctor Sloan.

Sloan was the son of a Baptist minister who had been raised with all the restrictions and religion that only the child of a Baptist minister has ever experienced. He came to Honolulu from a denominational college in Minneapolis, Minnesota where he had been head of the history department, and professor of mediaeval history. There he taught what they expected him to teach but his real interest was research. When he was forty he dropped out of academia hoping to retire in Hawaii, but soon learned that he had to go back to work. For a while he had been employed with one of the museums in Honolulu, and had started attending the First Aloha Christian Tabernacle because his wife wanted to.

When Pastor Bell learned of Sloan's religious childhood and academic background, he asked Sloan to teach an adult Sunday School class. He was an exciting teacher, and after the first quarter Sloan never had less than fifty or sixty in his class. Eventually Pastor

Bell asked him to join the staff as head of education with the idea that Sloan would set up a college level Bible school.

Because he was on the staff, taught in both the Bible school, and the adult Sunday school, and occasionally preached at one of the Sunday morning services, the congregation began referring to him as Pastor Sloan. But he was not a pastor, and never thought of himself as one. He had just sort of evolved into being associated professionally with the clergy. He didn't belong there, and he knew it, but somehow the opportunity never presented itself to where he could tell Pastor Bell that he wasn't really one of them. Besides, he needed the job, and the pay was better than he could have gotten from any museum.

When he joined the staff of the church Pastor Bell had apologized for the smallness of the office that was given to him. Even the youth pastor had a bigger office, but James Sloan was quite happy with it. On the other side of the back wall of his office was Pastor Bell's office. On one side was Doug Bautista's office, and on the other side was Don Bjork's office. It was the simplest thing in the world to just raise the panels of the false ceiling and reach over and plant a bug in their offices. Within a week he had the three offices bugged. He could record, or listen to what was said in those three offices to his heart's content. He knew more dirt about people in the congregation, and the staff, than anyone else. There was nothing he wanted to do with the information; he just liked knowing it. He would never have divulged what he knew to anyone including to those he knew about, but it amused him to hear someone speaking so piously when he knew the truth about them. He was in a hurry now to get to his office to hear what Pastor Bell and Doug were going to talk about. Pastor Bell had sounded very upset.

A young lady followed Don Bjork into his office and Doctor Sloan put in a tape to record what would be said in Bjork's office. He put another tape in another recorder to record what was said in Pastor Bell's office, and then put on earphones, and sat down at his desk. No one would think anything of his having earphones on his head. They were used to him listening to teaching tapes.

There was nothing much going on in Bell's office yet. He heard Bell dial the phone and he could just picture Bell leaning back in his high back executive chair with his right hand behind his head while the left hand held the phone to his ear. Bell had brown hair, which everyone knew was by *Grecian Formula.* Bell was talking to his travel agent about his trip to Singapore. Sloan was not interested in that, and he started looking over some student's papers his ears set to go into listening when the correct sound triggered it.

The knock on Bell's door triggered Sloan to listen. There was still only the voice of Bell talking to his agent, but he could just see him leaning forward in his chair, waving the person in, and then pointing to a chair for them to sit in.

"Well, Bev, I have to go now. See if you can arrange that, and get back to me on it," Bell said, and Sloan could even here the sound of the phone hanging up.

"You wanted to see me?" Doug asked.

"Yes, Doug. How could you have done that to me," Pastor Bell said starting right in without any small talk. "You have put me in a very awkward position. The first thing Yamamoto did when he saw the newscast last night was call me and ask when you had been made Senior Associate Pastor, and why hadn't he been told about it. This makes me look bad, Doug. Here he is State Superintendent, and an associate pastor like everyone else, and you are suddenly a Senior Associate Pastor?"

Sloan could visualize Bell leaning forward in his chair, his arms resting parallel with the edges of the blotter on is desk as he asked the challenging question.

"Now," Bell went on, "I can either make a statement to the congregation, and to the rest of the staff that you are not a senior associate which will make them ask why you said you were when you weren't. Or I can say that you are a senior associate, which will raise questions with some of the rest of the staff, particularly Pastor Yamamoto, as to why. Either way you have put me in an embarrassing position, and made me look bad. I have no idea why you could have said such a thing since we have never discussed it. You know, Doug, that my policy has always been that everybody is an associate pastor with the same rank and pay. Pastors have different responsibilities, but the same rank. To give one pastor a higher rank would imply that I think one ministry is more important than another. They are all important in the work of the Kingdom. You've known that, Doug. Why did you do this to me?"

"I have a letter I would like you to read, Pastor Bell," Doug said. "I think it will explain everything."

"Read it to me," Pastor Bell said, and Sloan could just see Bell leaning back in his chair looking up at the ceiling this time with both hands clasped behind his head. Having someone read their own letter, or memo was a trait of Bell's. Many times when Sloan had taken in a memo of one kind or another, Pastor Bell would lean back and say, "Read it to me." Sloan was not sure whether Bell did that because he didn't read very well, or because he knew reading something aloud often made the reader change the way things were said.

Doug began to read.

Dear Pastor Bell,

Let me say at the outset how much I appreciate all you have done for me. You have been like a father to me. You were the one that baptized our two sons, and Beverly and I have the highest regard for you: as a mentor, a friend, our pastor, and a man of God. I am very thankful for the opportunities that you have given me.

"However, I feel that I am no longer being challenged in the work environment of the Church. For the past three years I have had the three major responsibilities of: one; being your administrative assistant, two; business manager for the church and three; land acquisition and fund raising for the new church. In addition I have the standard pastoral responsibilities of which you are aware.

"Although you have given me these responsibilities, you have not really given me the authority that should go with them. The rest of the staff, for example, do not really think that when I say something in your absence that I am speaking for you. Consequently in many cases I am not only hampered in accomplishing what you want done, but actually opposed.

"Because of that I have been making inquiries in the secular arena, and have been offered a position with responsibility and authority. It is a position that will challenge my training, and experience. As you may expect the salary is also somewhat higher than I am currently getting here. If I were to accept this position, I would of course continue to attend this church, to support you in all you do, and help and minister in any way I could as a layperson.

"Going someplace else is not, however, my first choice. I would much prefer to stay right here, but in order to do that I would have to have the position of Senior Associate Pastor. That is so that when I say something people will know that I am their superior, that I am speaking for you, and that I have the authority to demand, and get, their compliance with your desires when I voice them.

"In addition I would need a salary increase of ten percent. That salary would be appropriately commensurate with the responsibilities of the new position though still less than I am being offered elsewhere.

"I want to thank you again for all you have done, and I hope that

23

whatever you decide, you will know that I will always be a member of this church, and totally supportive of you and your programs."

There was a pause and Sloan heard Pastor Bell ask, "Is that it?"

"Well I signed it of course."

It was, Sloan thought, a good letter. Bautista had analyzed Bell perfectly, which wasn't that hard to do. Bell was from West Texas and had started preaching at sixteen before he was out of high school. Doctor James Sloan admired the man. He had, as it was said in the military, "come up through the ranks" to become senior pastor of one of the largest churches in Honolulu. He had in his rise from one church to the next taken night and correspondence classes so he had eventually earned his degree. He had also learned all the necessary social graces by studying etiquette books so that some diplomat meeting him at a banquet would not have known that he did not have a formal education, or a 'good' family background. He had also learned how to be a consummate politician.

A secular politician has to worry about his constituents, and supporters, really only while he is campaigning. Once he is elected he has a job guaranteed pretty much for the length of the term, and if he has not done anything drastically wrong, will as the incumbent, probably be elected again. It is almost assured. But to be a successful pastor one must be a shrewd politician at all times with the ability to walk the fine line of persuading and controlling the people yet not offending them. Say or do something that offends someone, and they will go to some other church taking what they put in the offering plate with them.

Douglas Bautista had Pastor Bell over the barrel. Everyone knew that Doug had grown up in the church. Most of them, the old-timers especially, all knew that it had always been Doug's dream to be a pastor in the church where he had grown up. He said it often enough. Every time he had a chance to preach he reminded the congregation that he had grown up in the church. He would tell them that it had been his dream, and his prayer, to be a pastor in the church where he grew up, and how good God was to have answered that prayer.

If Pastor Doug were to go to some other church, or even start a church of his own, the congregation would have all solemnly nodded their heads and said that Pastor Doug was answering the call of God. But to go and work in the world was a drastic step that could only be the result of something terrible. They would all think Pastor Bell must have really done something wrong to make Pastor Doug give up his lifelong dream. But, of course, Pastor Doug was too saintly a person to ever tell anyone what Pastor Bell had done.

For Doug to continue attending the church would prove to the people what a saint he was, and would also always keep the question of 'Why?' alive. Sloan had no doubt that Doug would get what he was asking for. At least he would get the title, if not the raise, and the title was what Doug really wanted.

"What firm are you thinking of going with?" Pastor Bell asked.

"Hawaii Pacific Resource and Development."

"But, Doug, why did you have to go and proclaim your promotion on television before even discussing it with me. And especially under those terrible circumstances of a dead woman at our door. What am I going to do about Brother Yamamoto?"

"Make him a Senior Associate Pastor too," Doug said, and Sloan knew that Doug did not consider Yamamoto of any consequence as a pastor or a man.

Yamamoto was a house painter who had been the first student in Pastor Melvin's Aloha Bible School. The first year the school was in operation Yamamoto had been the only student. At the end of the second year he was licensed to preach. Yamamoto had been in the same place, at the same church for the past fifty years. Now by virtue of longevity, Yamamoto was elected Superintendent of Hawaii's Aloha Christian Tabernacles every year. Superintendent was mostly an honorary position, which no one else really wanted. Although Yamamoto was listed as one of the staff of the First Aloha Christian Tabernacle, three fourths of his salary came from the state association.

Sloan shook his head and smiled a little. That was very shrewd of Doug. By making two people senior associate pastors Pastor Bell could not be accused of favoritism and Yamamoto was no threat to Doug. Yamamoto was a sixty-five year old man who claimed he got up at three every morning to pray for an hour, and then did fifty push-ups.

"Well, give me your letter and let me pray about it."

"I have to know soon. I have to let H.P.R & D know whether or not I'm joining them."

"I understand, Doug. I'll let you know as soon as I've decided."

Sloan heard Doug leave the office, and switched to the mike that was Don Bjork's office hoping to hear some juicy gossip, but Bjork was just finishing praying for the woman's sick mother. He was surprised to hear a knock on his door, and when he looked that direction saw Doug's outline through the rippled glass. The glass was such that you could see what people were doing on the other side, but not clearly see their features.

"Come in, Doug," Sloan said taking off his earphones. "I was just listening to a Paul Ramakin teaching. Have you heard him?"

"No," Doug said sitting down. "Is he good?"

"Depends what you mean by 'good'. He's an effective speaker. But I don't agree with everything he says. But I don't think that's what you came into talk to me about, is it, Doug?"

"I was in talking to Pastor Bell this morning. He wanted to talk to me about some changes in the staff that he's thinking of making—"

"Well, I'm sure most of us are aware of some of those changes," Sloan said interrupting him. "After all it was announced over the body of a naked girl. I mean, really, Doug, I've heard of Madison Avenue using sex to get people's attention when they want to make a statement, but does the church have to use their methods? And isn't using a dead, naked, girl going a little too far even for Madison Avenue?"

Doug smiled a little not knowing exactly how to take Sloan's remark. "It just came out that way. Actually Pastor is making both Brother Yamamoto a senior associate pastor too. I guess it's because both of us in our own way have been with the church longer than anyone else. But he wanted me to tell you that this has nothing to do with the Education Department. These changes have nothing to do with you, or the departments under you."

"What departments will they affect?"

"Well, when you put it that way," Doug said with a shrug, "none I guess."

"Well, then. Congratulations! Is that in order?"

"Well, yes. Thank you," he said getting up.

Doug left closing the door behind him, and Sloan saw him standing outside Don's door and went back to listening to Don's office. He heard Doug enter and say, "Don, at the next staff meeting Pastor Bell is going to announce that I am Senior Associate Pastor. If there should be any discussion, or opposition from any of the others you'll support me in this, won't you?"

"Yeah, I guess," Don said.

"There shouldn't be any guess about it, Don."

"Sure, Doug. Of course I'll support you."

CHAPTER FOUR

Jacqueline Marqueoff was awake before she opened her eyes. Slowly and painfully things began to come back to her. She remembered the newscast and tears began to form behind her closed eyelids when she thought of the picture of Susan. Slowly the whole horror of knowing Susan was dead flooded in on her. She remembered going with Kimo and Marcella to their apartment. They had tried to get her to eat a little and had given her some herbal tea.

Marcella had sat up talking to her, though Jackie couldn't remember what they talked about. She remembered that they had talked about Cynthia and Susan, but she couldn't remember what else. She had been so tired that she had been unable to go to sleep. It was after midnight when Marcella had given her a sleeping pill. She guessed that she must have fallen asleep about one in the morning, which would have been three in the morning San Francisco time.

She thought that she must still be in their apartment because she did not remember going back to her own. There was a dusty smell in the air like the smell of leaves in autumn, and a rhythmic rattling sound that she couldn't identify. She was awake, but her body felt too tired to move. She wished she could go back to sleep, but the urge to go to the bathroom kept her awake.

She was lying on her side and she opened the eye that was not pressed against the pillow. The room looked different in the daylight. She realized that she was on the bed that was in the living room, which was where she and Marcella had been sitting most of the evening. It had been full of pillows so it could be used as a couch. There were a couple of director's chairs in the room. They were now full of the pillows that had been on the couch. But mostly the floor of the room was covered with something that looked like thin palm fronds. On the other side of the room Kimo was sitting cross-legged on the floor weaving the fronds into a mat.

She sat up dropping her legs over the edge of the bed and ran both hands, fingers spread, shaking her hands as she pushed them up through her thick, brown-blond hair. As she did, Kimo looked up at her. She had a headache, and her eyes were burning, but mostly she just felt tired.

"You OK, yeah?" He asked looking up.

27

"I guess so," she said getting up. "What time is it?"

"Bout ten," he said getting up from the floor. "Wad-da-wan? Coffee? Tea? I fix for you"

"Oh, don't bother," she said heading toward the door.

"Aye, it's no bother. Seestah say I take you see Kunayoshi this morning."

"Oh no. I couldn't ask you to do that." Right then she didn't want to think about Kunayoshi. All she wanted to do was give into her grief, but she knew she had to take care of the unhappy business of making arrangements for claiming Susan's body, arranging for taking the body back to San Francisco, and most important of all, find out who killed both her sisters.

"What? You know where his office is? You gonna take one taxi all over? Marcella say I drive you. She plenty huhu bout Cindy. Cindy an Seestah good friends. Use to go out together. Sometimes Cindy use to help out in the shop. So what you want? Coffee or what?"

"Just let me go freshen up a bit and then we'll talk about it."

"OK. I fix breakfast. Just go shee-shee and wash the face then come back. We eat breakfast then get all dress for go see Kunayoshi."

* * *

All the offices were exactly the same with two plate glass windows and a door with a window. The walls holding the windows and doors did not go all the way to the ceiling so there was an incomprehensible hum in the air that implied that something was being accomplished. The only difference was the names on the doors. A red fire extinguisher hanging waist high under the windows of every third office punctuated the stark white and glass of the hallway between the two lines of offices.

Inside Kunayoshi's office the walls were decorated with misty Japanese prints. In the center of a shoulder-high file cabinet was a two-foot high doll of a samurai warrior. The receptionist that showed them there knocked, and then opened the door for them to enter. Kunayoshi stood up perfunctorily asking them to sit down, and then sat down again himself. He shuffled a couple of papers on his desk, and then looked up just lifting his head a little from his hunched over position at his desk. He sat with his hands folded on his desktop. He sat looking at her in a bored sort of way never changing the expression on his face. He wore round, black-framed glassed that magnified his eyes, and sitting there with his magnified eyes, he looked like a frog. Jacqueline didn't like Kunayoshi. It was not his looks she didn't like, but she sensed a hostility that she didn't feel was warranted.

"I've had half a dozen people in here today telling me who the dead woman was," Kunayoshi said. "Who do you say she was?"

He was wearing a white aloha shirt with ink line designs of Hawaiian canoes, sailing ships and charts. She liked the shirt, but thought that it didn't look right on him.

"The woman we are talking about is my cousin." She said pushing her right hand through thick, brown-blond hair on the right side of her face.

She expected some sign of sympathy, but he just kept staring at her.

"Her name is Susan Harcourt and she is twenty-three years of age."

"And what is your name?"

"Jacqueline Marqueoff."

"Where do you live, Ms. Marqueoff?"

"San Francisco."

"How long have you been in Honolulu?"

"I arrived a little after noon yesterday."

"You can confirm that, I suppose?"

"Eh! What all da kine wit her. I see her come yestahday wit da kine luggage," Kimo said standing up. His large bulk leaned menacingly over the desk.

"And who are you?" Kunayoshi asked totally unintimidated by Kimo's size, or voice.

"Kimo Kahikokane," Kimo said sitting down.

"Did you know the dead woman too?"

"We neighbahs."

"Where were you the night before last, Kimo?"

"I home."

"All alone?"

"Eh! Unreal, Man," Kimo said jumping up again. "My seestah. She know I home all night. You wanna ass me moe question you get me one lawyah." He stood there for a moment, and then sat down when Kunayoshi looked back at Jacqueline.

"What do you do for a living, Ms. Marqueoff?"

"Online trading mostly and some website design."

29

"You're a stock broker?" He asked the question with a tone that indicated he was suspicious of all on-line traders.

"Well, I am a member of the San Francisco Stock Exchange, and sometimes people give me money to invest for them, but mostly I just buy and sell on line."

"And what brought you to Honolulu?"

"My sister, my cousin actually, but we grew up together so we always referred to each other as sisters, had been calling me every night, and then when she stopped, and didn't answer her phone I came to see what had happened to her. Can you tell me what happened to her? Do you know how she died?

"We know how she died," he said matter-of-factly.

"How?"

"I'm not permitted to divulge that information just yet."

"The television said she appeared to be poisoned. Was she?"

"As I said, we can't divulge that information."

"Can't divulge it, or don't you know yet," she said getting angry. She stood up frustrated and finding it hard to control her anger. "You people are as sloppy about this as you were about what killed my other sister. You said it was an overdose. An overdose of what? You wouldn't believe those that said Cynthia didn't use drugs. She may have been an exhibitionist, but she was also a health nut. She didn't smoke, drink, or eat red meats, and never used drugs. Her only vice was a love for Coca-Cola.

"Then when Susan comes back to find out who killed her sister because you sons-of-bitches can't do it, she is murdered, and you have the nerve to tell me you can't tell me how she died. Well I'll help you out with your job. She was murdered because she was getting too close to the truth about who murdered Cynthia."

She had been able to control her emotions until then, but she suddenly broke down and ran from his office sobbing with Kimo right behind her. They got to the car, and sat there until she had control of herself again and she said, "I think I'd like to go to the church now. Do you know where it is?"

"I know the place. We go."

He stayed in the car while she walked around the front of the church, and stood for a moment looking at the place where Susan had lain. She looked around taking in the arrangement of the trees, and hedge, and walls, and then climbed the steps to the offices. A gray haired lady smiled cheerfully as she entered. "May I help you?" she asked.

"Would it be possible to talk with Pastor Bautista?"

"He's in a meeting right now. Do you have an appointment?"

"No. My name is Jacqueline Marqueoff. The woman he found on the steps yesterday morning was my sister. I was hoping I might talk to him."

"I'm so sorry to hear that, Ms. Marqueoff," she said seeming genuinely moved. "Won't you have a seat. I'll see if he can leave the meeting," and then added, "I'm sure he can."

"Thank you," Jackie said sitting down in the chair closest to the receptionist.

The sweet, gray-haired lady picked up the phone, and pressed a couple of buttons. "Momi, there's a Ms. Marqueoff out here that wants to talk to Pastor Doug," the receptionist said. "She says she's the sister of the woman he found on the steps yesterday—Yeah—OK." She hung up the phone, and rose up a little to see over the counter, and said, "He'll be with you in just a minute."

A woman approached from the direction of the hall with her hand extended saying, "Ms. Marqueoff, I'm Momi Cadrino, Pastor Bautista's secretary. I'm so sorry about your sister. We all are."

She was an attractive, dark haired, big-busted woman wearing a muumuu. Jackie saw Momi eyeing her clothes enviously as she stood up, and Jackie was glad she had worn the tan suit. They shook hands, and the woman said, "Would you follow me please," and started down the hall ahead of her.

Walking down the hall Jackie tried to see through the rippled glass of the windows, and read the names on each door as she walked by. Each door had simulated wood plaques with white lettering. The first one on the left was DONALD BJORD and beneath it; SINGLES PASTOR. Directly across from it was DAMIEN PASQUAL and beneath it; YOUTH PASTOR. They were followed by DR. JAMES SLOAN, DIR. OF EDUCATION on the left and BETTY CLIPPER; MUSIC MINISTER on the right. Momi opened the last door on the left and held it for her, and then closed it behind her.

Pastor Bautista stood up as she entered coming around his desk with his hand extended. "I'm sorry, Ms. Marqueoff, very sorry about your sister," he said shaking hands with her. "If there is anything we can do to help we're here for you." He smiled a professionally sympathetic smiled, and then asked her to sit down. He walked around the desk to his chair.

She eyed him critically. This was the man that told the reporters that he didn't know Susan, and yet his name and telephone number

31

was on Susan's yellow sheets of paper. She had asked to see him because his was the only name she knew at the church, but she didn't trust him. She thought he was thinner than he had looked on television, but he was still a short, chunky, sleazy looking man that she just couldn't trust.

"Now, how can I help you?" he asked in a very business-like way which implied he would try to help if he could, but he wanted to get it over with.

"Well I don't know exactly, but the police don't seem to know very much, or they just don't want to be helpful. They won't even tell me how Susan died. I thought since you found the body maybe other people had contacted you, and you might know something that might help me. Did the police say anything to you about how she might have died?"

"No, I'm afraid that I can't help you there at all."

"I just don't know where to turn. I feel so frustrated and lost. I just arrived from San Francisco yesterday, and when I get to her apartment my sister is not there, and the first news I have of her is on television. I just don't know what to do." She knew she sounded pathetic. She intended to sound that way, but at the same time she really didn't know where to turn.

"I understand. Death is always hard to comprehend, and an unexpected death is even more emotionally devastating. Are any other members of your family here?"

"No," she said dabbing at the tears that were genuine but which she also permitted. "I found a list with the names of some people on it among Susan's things. Some were just names without addresses or phone numbers. This is a big church, and I thought maybe you might know some of these people. Do you know a John S, I, U," she asked spelling the name. "How do you pronounce that?"

"That's pronounced 'See-you' and no I don't know a John Siu."

"What about Bucky Smith?"

He shook his head.

"Marvin Hall?"

"That name sounds familiar for some reason, but—" he opened his hands in a gesture of futility.

"What about Manuel Rodriguez?"

"No," he shook his head and pursed his lips, "I don't know any Manuel Rodriguez."

"Clarence Ching?"

"Yes, I know a Clarence Ching. But I don't think he knew your

32

sister. There are a lot of Clarence Chings in Honolulu. The one I know is about twenty-three, single and very active in our Singles Fellowship."

"May I have his address and telephone number?"

"Well, we don't usually give out that information, but under the circumstances I guess I can give it to you. I don't think you'll learn anything from him, and I would appreciate it if you would not tell him you got his number from me," he said reaching for the Church directory. He gave her the number and address, and said, "Is there anything else I can do for you."

"Well, it's an awfully big favor, and I'm sort of embarrassed by it—"

"Go ahead."

"I blew up at Detective Kunayoshi today before I had asked him when I could claim my sister's body." The tears came to her eyes, and Bautista took a box of Kleenex from a drawer and handed it across the desk to her. "I don't want to go back there. I wonder if you could call him, or the police, or whoever it is takes care of these things, and let me know when I can claim my sister? I can't really make the arrangements to take her home until I know when I can get her."

"I understand. Certainly. I'd be glad to do that for you."

"You can reach me at 523-2783. That's the number at my sister's apartment. Or you can call me on my cell at area code 415-289-7335. I really do appreciate it."

"Don't mention it. Do you have any friends in Honolulu?"

"Not really," she said pushing her hand through her hair again.

"We have our midweek service tonight. Why don't you join us? I'll be there, and I can introduce you around. Meet some people you might find interesting so you're not so alone in this city."

"Thank you. I might just do that," she said knowing full well she wouldn't.

He stood up indicating that the meeting was at an end, and he held the door for her. As she left she saw the plaques under the window in his door: PASTOR DOUGLAS BAUTISTA and under that: ADMINISTRATIVE ASSISTANT and a third plaque: DIRECTOR OF DEVELOPMENT.

* * *

She was just getting out of the shower when she heard her phone ringing. She wrapped a towel around herself and answered it.

"Is this Jacqueline Marqueoff?"

"Yes."

"You don't know who I am, but I thought you might like to know that Douglas Bautista has a cousin named Manuel Rodriquez. He's a foreman for a construction company," the voice said, and then the caller hung up.

CHAPTER FIVE

They spent the earlier part of the morning with Kimo driving her around to various mortuaries so she could find out which offered the best services. It was not something she had felt she could do over the phone. While riding around she had come to the conclusion that the person that had called her the evening before must be from the church. She was certain that the only person she had mentioned Manuel Rodriguez to was Reverend Bautista, and he had claimed not to know anyone by that name. Yet how could anyone have heard her mention the name to Bautista?

There hadn't been anyone in the room so she must have mentioned it to someone else without knowing she did it. No matter how hard she searched her brain she could not remember to whom she might have mentioned Rodriguez. In her mind she relived the whole day, and there was no one she mentioned him to, but she must have.

It was around 11:30 when she got home, and there was a message on the machine from Kunayoshi asking her to call him. When she did, he said she could go to the police station, and identify, and claim Susan's body whenever she wished. He pointed out that she would have to bring some kind of documentation showing that they were related in order to claim the body. After that the mortuary with which she had made arrangements could then come and get Susan.

It was all just too frustrating. She didn't know if she had any papers with her that showed they were related. It seemed that everything was closing in on her. It would have been stressful enough just to have to make the funeral arrangements, but with everything else she had on her mind it was more than she could handle right at the moment. She lay down on the bed, and started to cry trying not to cry too loudly so that Kimo wouldn't come around trying to comfort her. She appreciated all that Kimo and Marcella had done, but right now she just wanted to be alone, and have a good cry.

She had no idea when the crying changed to sleeping, but it was almost one in the afternoon when she woke up feeling hot and sticky. She got out of the dress she had fallen asleep in, and went and took a shower. When she came out she was feeling relaxed and alert. She called the church remembering the names on the plaques in the hall, and was able to get an appointment with Pastor Bjork at three, and one with Dr. Sloan at three-thirty. She didn't know what they could tell her, but she was certain that it had to be someone from the church that had called to tell her about Bautista and Rodriguez.

She got dressed in a split-skirt tan suit with shoes and purse that exactly matched the suit. She got Kimo to drive her to the airport Alamo office where she had reserved a car. Kimo protested saying she could borrow his car anytime she wished, but she insisted.

She got her car, and drove to the Ala Moana shopping center, looking mostly at the early Christmas decorations, until it was time to go to the church. When the cheery, gray-haired receptionist called to let him known Jacqueline was there, Pastor Bjork came out, and took her back to his office himself.

Bjork was a large, tall man that might have played end for some football team. He had a lumbering walk that suggested he belonged on a farm somewhere rather than in a church office. He had red hair and a round, freckled face that would have been babyish if it wasn't for a scar that ran the length of his face from his right cheekbone to his jawbone. He waited for her to sit down, and then sat sideways at his desk.

"I am very sorry about your sister. I didn't know her, but you have my deepest sympathy," he said, and even as he said it he had a gentle, reassuring smile on his face.

"She was actually my cousin. Her parents died when she was five, and she and her sister came to live with us. I was ten at the time, and we grew up together. We always thought of each other as sisters. Do you think she might at any time been at your singles group?"

"I don't remember her. Of course I don't know for sure. She might have been there once or twice, and I just don't remember her. We do have quite a large singles group. The only picture I've seen of her was what I saw on television, and she didn't look at all familiar to me," he said all this while at the same time nervously picking at his wristwatch with his right hand.

"Oh, I have a recent picture of her. Actually it's of all three of us," she said going into her purse.

It was a picture that had been taken just before Cynthia and Susan had taken their vacation to Hawaii, As she went through her wallet looking for the picture Jackie wondered if Kunayoshi would accept the picture as sufficient documentation to let her claim Susan's body.

She handed Bjork the picture and said, "The one on the left is

36

Susan. The one on the right is my other cousin, Cynthia."

He shook his head. "No. I can't say that I ever saw the one on the left, except of course on the news." He paused for a moment and then said, "but I've seen the one on the right." For some reason he suddenly seeming more relaxed.

"You have?" Jackie asked startled.

"Well, I think I have. Only saw her once though, at the church's Fourth of July picnic. At least I think it was her."

"Well, if she was at the picnic then there must have been someone there that knew her."

"I don't think she was actually at the picnic. I think she was with Pastor Doug's cousin. Your sister and the man she was with were at the beach. Walking to their car from the beach they saw Pastor Doug, and came over to say hello."

"What was his name?"

"I don't know for sure. Manny I think. But Doug has so many cousins no one can keep up with them all. I only know the ones that attend this church."

"How many of them attend the church?"

"Quite a few. And then he has a lot of relatives I've never seen. His parents and grandparents attend here. Three brothers, and their wives, and children, and two unmarried sisters."

"Manny doesn't attend this church then?"

"No. He doesn't attend any church that I know of."

"How could I get a hold of this Manny?"

"Pastor Bautista should know his address and phone number. After all they are cousins."

"Pastor Bjork, I see from your diplomas that you have a Masters in Psychology. Do you do a lot of counseling?"

"I probably do more counseling than all the other Pastor on the staff put together. That's actually why I'm here and what like to do best. I hope to go back to school next year to finish work on my Doctorate in Clinical Psychology."

"Here in Hawaii?"

"Oh, no. In Seattle. University of Washington. I've been offered a position as Director of Counseling with a Catholic human services institution. While there I hope to complete my doctorate."

"Tell me, Pastor Bjork, since you're trained in these areas, why would someone kill a person, and leave the nude body on the church steps?"

"I don't know," he said raising a freckled hand to seriously and contemplatively rub his chin. "Only a sick mind would do something like that. I know that's a cop-out answer, but then only a sick mind would kill someone in the first place. Did they do it to embarrass the church? Did they do it as an act of defiance? Did they do it to throw suspicion one direction or another? I really don't know. I don't think anyone does," he said, paused for a moment and then went on. "How long have you been here, Miss Marqueoff?"

"I arrived the day before yesterday."

"The very day your cousin was—" he paused, and she had expected him to say 'killed' but he said, "found?"

"Yes. I learned about it on the evening news."

"What a horrible experience that must have been for you? What made you come to Hawaii right at this time anyway?"

"I was concerned about my sister."

"Concerned? Any special reason why you were concerned?"

"We've always been very close, and when she stopped calling me, and I got no answer when I called her I became concerned. I'll admit that I thought maybe she had just gone off to one of the other islands with somebody and forgotten to tell me she was going to be gone. I thought that when she got back we would have a big fight about it. I would accuse her of being inconsiderate, and causing me to spend all kinds of money to come to Hawaii, and she would have shouted at me about interfering in her life. I certainly didn't expect what I found."

"No. I can imagine. Do you remember what your last conversation with your cousin was about?"

"It was nothing special. Just normal sister chit-chat."

"Did she say anything that might have caused you to be concerned, or worried?"

"I don't think so. Just normal chatter."

"Well at least it was pleasant, and it is always nice to have a pleasant last memory," he said, and she thought that the expression on his face somehow relaxed as though he had been concerned about something.

"Yeah, I guess so," she said.

"How long do you expect to stay in Hawaii?"

"I don't know exactly," she said pushing a hand up through her brown-blond hair. "I have to get Susan's things in order, and arrange for taking her back to San Francisco. Right now I'm waiting for some papers from home that will show I was related to Susan so I can claim her body."

"Bureaucracies can be hard to deal with sometimes. But I guess they have their rules too."

"I guess so." There was a pause and she said, "Well, Pastor Bjork, I really do appreciate your seeing me. Thank you for all your help, and your encouragement."

"Any time I can help in any way, don't hesitate to call," he said standing up. "We have a wonderful singles group here on Friday nights. We start at seven. Come a little early and I'll introduce you around. It's always nice to have friends when you arrive in a new place."

She thought it a little strange that both Bautista, and Bjork had said something about it being nice to have friends when you arrived in a new place, and she wondered if that was just a line they used to get people to come to the church. Both of them had mentioned a church service.

"Thank you. I'll see how it goes. Don't bother walking me out. I have an appointment to see Doctor Sloan next. I'll just wait out in the lobby until it's time. I know I'm early."

He walked her to the reception area anyway; talking and smiling congenially, and then left her. Doctor Sloan came out almost immediately as though he knew somehow that she was finished with her appointment with Pastor Bjork. He was easily as tall as Pastor Bjork, and looked exactly like what he was, someone who had once been athletic, and had let himself go. He had the beginnings of a middle age paunch, but still walked with the smoothness of one who never lost his footing whether on the side of a mountain, or on a ship's deck. His dark hair, which was cut short as though he didn't want to be bothered caring for it, was beginning to gray. She followed him into his office, and he pointed to a chair for her as he sat down.

"Well, Ms. Marqueoff you seem to be wanting to talk to everybody today," he said.

"Since my sister was found on this church's steps I'm trying to find someone who might have known her. Might have been with her just before she died, might be able to explain why she died the way she did."

"And how did she die?" he asked turning to his desk and writing on a scrap of paper as he asked the question.

"The police haven't categorically said it, but they left me with the impression that she was poisoned."

"And you want to know why," he said holding up the piece of

paper. On it was written –Do you know where the Ala Moana Shopping Center is?

She looked perplexed and then said, "Yes, I know—"

He held a finger to his lips indicating she was not to say anything, and started to write again. When he held the piece of paper up it said—Meet me at the Food Court in fifteen minutes.

"I'm sorry, but I don't think there is anyone here that can help you, Miss Marqueoff," he said standing up abruptly, and putting the sheets of paper into the shredder.

She stood up frowning a little, and he held the door for her as she went out ahead of him.

As he passed the front desk he said to the receptionist, "I'm leaving for the day, Karen. I'm going to the printers, and then home."

He caught up with her as she was getting into her car. "I'll meet you in the section close to the fountain," he said.

She looked at him not knowing what to ask him, or what to think of him. He was bizarre and she wondered if he was a little off. But she had to find out something about Susan and she was certain that the Food Court would be crowded enough that she would not be in any danger. For all of his strange actions he did appear to be harmless.

When she got to Ala Moana Shopping Center she found him seated at a table with two drinks in front of him. He picked up the drinks and walked toward her. He handed her one of the drinks, and jerking his head a little said, "Come on."

She followed him to his car. He held the door for her to get in. "Where are we going?" she asked hesitating.

"Just across the street to the park. You can take your car if you like." She got in; and he closed the door behind her, and walked around to his side and got in. "If I had tried to explain it back in the office it would have taken too long," he said starting the car. "Hope you like diet Coke. I didn't know what you liked. Don't much like diet Coke myself, but that was what my wife drank and so that was what I always ordered for her. It got to be a habit, and I still do it."

"This is fine."

He drove out of the parking lot and across the street to Ala Moana Park. They walked out to Magic Island. Already the joggers; men in shorts, and women wearing spandex, were making the rounds of the asphalt jogging trails, and she thought of how odd she must look walking along in a suit, high heels, and with a coke in one hand. They sat down on a bench overlooking the channel to the yacht harbor. He sat sideways with his long legs crossed, and one arm along the back of the bench looking off across the water as though she wasn't there and he was talking to someone else.

"I'm the one that called you last night, and told you about Doug's cousin, Manuel. Everyone calls him Manny. I heard Doug deny knowing him when you said the name, but he knows Manuel Rodriguez all right."

"You mean to tell me those walls are that thin?" she asked.

"No," he said, pursed his lips and shook his head a little.

"Then how did you know I asked him about it?"

He turned, looked her right in the eyes, and she noticed for the first time the soft greenness of his eyes which made what he said that much more startling. "I have his office bugged."

"What?" she said genuinely shocked. She said it so loud that she almost shouted it.

He smiled pleased with the effect that remark had on her. "And you are the only one that knows. Even my wife never knew. She would never have permitted it. I told you so that you will know that I am being up front with you. I called you last night to see what you would do. If you had not pursued it, I would have figured you didn't really care, that you were just going through some motions, and I would have let it go. But since you are pursuing it, I'll tell you everything I know and help you any way I can. Now, why was your sister," he shook his head a little, and then corrected himself, "your cousin Susan here?"

"She had come back to see if she could find out how her sister, Cynthia, died."

"Did she find anything?"

"I don't really know." She was about to tell him about the letter, and then held off.

"I heard you ask Doug yesterday about getting your sister's body released. Did you have any luck there?"

"Kunayoshi called this morning and said I could claim the body if I had proof that I was related to her."

"Let me tell you something about this town. It is a city with a population of a million or so people, but it is really just a provincial, chauvinistic, small town with a small town mentality. Everybody is related to everybody else and it is a closed shop. Bautista for example has relatives everywhere; police force, water department, sanitation department, City Hall, State House, you name it he has a relative there who can get dirt on someone. But that also means that someone else has relatives everywhere who can get dirt on him, so

41

they keep a check on each other, and keep everyone else out. The whole state, from the governor to the lowest cop on the force, is on the take.

"Now Pastor Bell is on a big building program. He is from West Texas by way of California, and he's smart enough to know that he needs a local to deal with the locals, probably because Doug told him that, and so Doug Bautista is Director of Development. He gets a kickback on everything the church pays the architectural firms, the engineering consultants, the decorators, and on, and on. The company that gets the building contract will be the one that pays Bautista the most. Whether or not Bell knows about it, I don't know. But that's the way things are done here. The city sets aside land for affordable housing, and some Japanese developer comes along and pays every councilman something under the table, and suddenly he has permits to build a resort, and golf course.

"But the visitor doesn't want to know about these things, and why should they. They have paid their hard earned money to come to paradise, and that is what they should get. But you didn't come to enjoy paradise. You came to be involved in the sordid side of Hawaii. So you might as well know the truth of what you're up against. It is not going to be easy for you. Let me give you an example.

"About fifty, sixty years, ago a dance instructor named Lisa Au went suddenly missing on her way home after teaching a night dance class. There was a massive search on to find her. They finally found her body, and determined that she had been murdered. As soon as there started to be some indications that a police officer was involved in the murder the investigation ground to a halt. Inside Edition even did a segment on it. That murder has never been solved, and probably never will be.

"Now Kunayoshi wasn't about to tell you anything, or let you have anything. But one call from Doug, and suddenly Kunayoshi gives you what you want. You have to ask yourself, why was Pastor Bautista so eager to help you? My guess is that he wants you out of here. He wants you to claim your sister's body, and get back to the mainland."

"Then you think he is involved?" she asked looking at him sideways, her blue eyes showing her suspicion.

"I really don't know," he said nodding slightly, but seriously. "We do know that he denied knowing Manny. Now why would he do that? So I think he may be involved, but just how, or how much I don't know. That's what we'll have to find out."

"We?"

"I would think from what I've told you so far you would begin to understand that I want to help you."

"Why?"

"Well, there's lots of reasons. First I guess it is the challenge of it. I've been eavesdropping on the people around me for years, but I could never use what I heard. Nor did I ever really want to. I would never use it for blackmail, or anything of that nature, but now I can put what I've learned to good use.

"Secondly I want to get Doug. Everyone in the office except Momi, and Pastor Bell, hate his guts. He's an arrogant, slimy, deceitful, cruel little son-of-a-bitch, and I want to see him brought down." A hardness came into his green eyes when he said that.

"Boy you don't sound very much like a preacher."

"I'm not a preacher. I'm what some might call an egghead. That gives me the right to be angry about things. Where do you think all the protest of the sixties really started? In the colleges by people like me," he said smiling mischievously.

"Doug is a bully. He never picked on me directly. He would say cutting things to my wife when I wasn't around which would hurt her terribly, and he got at me by hurting her, and I couldn't get back at him. I want to bring him down like you wouldn't believe. If for no other reason to make up for all the hurt he caused my wife."

"Does your wife feel as you do?"

"She died a little over a year ago," he said brushing it off, and then went on. "I'll tell you something else. Doug has something on Don Bjork. I don't know what it is, but Doug uses it to get Don to do whatever he wants. Don didn't always acquiesce to Doug's demands. Make another appointment with Don Bjork. You had him talking to you. You might get him to tip his hand as to what Doug has on him. Now, is there anything else you would like to ask me?

"Yes, why did we come out here for this conversation?"

He smiled. "Well, it's like this. Human nature is such that we all attribute our own qualities, strengths and our weakness, to other people. A dishonest person believes that everyone is dishonest, and so trusts no one. An honest person thinks everyone is honest, and so trusts everyone. I have the three offices around me bugged, and so I assume that someone might just be trying to listen in on what I'm saying; especially if they think I'm talking about a murder in which they may have been involved. Besides, I like the water, and the sun, and watching the boats going in and out of the harbor."

"So then you do think that someone at the church murdered Susan?"

"I don't know if they murdered her, but someone there knows who did. Now I've told you about all I know. Is there something you should be telling me?"

"I don't know."

"I heard you discussing your sister Cynthia with Don. What have you learned about her?"

"Do you have all the offices bugged?"

"No. Just the ones on my side of the hall, Doug's, Don's and Pastor Bell's. But they are the important ones."

She shook her head in disbelief causing the brown-blond hair to swing back and forth. "Cynthia died a little over six weeks ago. The police claimed she died of an overdose of cocaine, but it wasn't the way they make it sound. Cynthia never used drugs. When we got her body home we had our family doctor arrange for an autopsy. What she died of was a heart attack caused by a reaction to the cocaine someone gave her without her knowing it. She would never have knowingly taken drugs. That's why Susan was here, to find out who gave Cynthia the drug that killed her. I think Susan died because she had discovered the truth of how Cynthia died."

"That's interesting. Six weeks ago you say?"

"Yes."

"That's just about the time that Doug was getting a lot of calls from Manny. When I say a lot there were two or three calls a day for a couple of days, and Doug made several calls to him. They were at night, and I had them on tape. Doug sounded angry, and upset with Manny, but I couldn't make out what it was about. I don't know if I still have those tapes, or not, or if I erased them. My guess is that since I couldn't make out what it was about I probably erased it, but I'll look and see if I still have them somewhere. See if there is anything we can make out from them. Anything else I should know?"

She reached into her purse, and took out the piece of paper with Susan's letter, and gave it to him.

He read it, and said, "Have you showed this to anyone else, or told anyone about it?"

"No!"

"Well don't. Don't show it to anyone, or tell anyone about it. And don't carry it with you. In fact get rid of it. Burn it."

"Why?"

44

"Because if somehow the 'him' that Susan is talking about should know about this message, he might also think that Susan told you who he is. You have been asking a lot of questions. If he thinks you are just curious, that is one thing, but if he thinks Susan told you who killed Cynthia then you may be next."

"Oh, My God! I never thought of that."

"Yeah, well, think about it. Your life, and more importantly to me now that I'm in this with you, my life may be on the line."

CHAPTER SIX

They sat on the lanai, Jackie had finally stopped calling it the balcony, with empty coffee cups in front of them looking out over the city. Marcella, who was not going to the shop until noon, had come by about eight-thirty and insisted Jackie join them for breakfast. Kimo was doing the cooking. It started with half a papaya, and then a plate of scrambled eggs, Portuguese sausage, and a pile of fried rice. It was the first time they had really sat down and talked.

Kimo and Marcella's parents owned the Hula supply store that Marcella managed. Although most of their clients were from the Hula Halaus, they were close enough to the Ala Moana shopping center that they had a good tourist trade. Marcella had graduated from the University of Hawaii with a degree in business administration and marketing and not only ran the business aspects of the store but all of the family's enterprises. They had bought the apartment in Makiki so that she would be close to the store. Most of the family lived Waimanolo side where they were all involved in supplying the store with genuine Hawaiian materials. They owned several acres of Ti plants. Ti leaves were big business. The leaves of Ti plant were used in everything from making authentic hula skirts to putting under an entree in the hotels. The leaves were picked daily by the younger children and were delivered to the hotels. For the halaus, the older children stripped the leaves and tied them into the skirts. All the dinner shows in Waikiki needed hula skirts. They also grew gourds for the Epo, and dyed the feathers for the Uli Uli. Kimo was the main weaver of Hala mats. He was proud of what he did. There were very few in Hawaii that still knew how to weave the genuine Hawaiian Hala mats. He had a passionate dislike for Filipinos mainly because of the cheap imitation mats they imported and passed off as Hawaiian. He lived with Marcella because the family didn't like her living alone Honolulu side.

Kimo and Marcella got to know Cindy soon after she moved in when Marcella's cat was lost. Marcella was going around to the neighbors asking if they had seen her cat. Cindy had joined her in the search. They found the cat two hours later lying twisted in the middle of the street three blocks away. A car had hit it. Marcella picked the cat up and carried it back to the apartment.

"Why foe you bring dat ting in heah, Woman? Trow in dumpstah. No bring in heah," Kimo said when they arrived at the door with the dead cat.

Marcella burst out crying. "I gonnah geev him decent funeral," she said slipping back into the Pidgin she grew up speaking.

Cindy had gone to Waimanolo with her, and helped her dig a grave under an Ulu tree next to where she had buried her dog ten years before. Marcella wasn't real sure of the exact spot, but it was somewhere there. Only the children, and Cindy stood next to her as she put the little box in the ground. The adults all shook their heads and said such things as "Why you do so dumb ting like dat foe?"

After that Cindy was part of the family. She was invited to all the luaus, and often helped out in the shop when an employee called in sick. She and Marcella went shopping together and out together. Many mornings and early afternoons before she had to go to work Cindy would sit drinking her Coke, or herbal tea, and talking to Kimo as he sat cross-legged on the floor weaving the hala.

It was not unusual for dancers to have men follow them from one club to the next. Some dancers might tell a customer they found attractive where they would go next that evening in the hopes that he would follow her, but most of the dancers tried to keep their rounds secret just to avoid being followed. But following a dancer wasn't that hard, and Cindy accepted being followed as part of the business. But if someone started pressuring her too much she would tell Kimo about it, and he would take her around from place to place pretending to be her 'man' until the other person stopped following her.

"Do you know of a Manuel, or a Manny Rodriguez?" Jackie asked Marcella.

"He one no good, bastad. I all de time tell Cindy no go wit heem. He all da time geev me da stinkeye. Ah one day gonna broke his face," Kimo exclaimed from where he was sitting on the floor inside.

"She did go out with him then?"

"He took her to a couple of Rainbow games and a fight or two. They went out occasionally," Marcella said. "There was nothing there as far as she was concerned. He is good looking, and has a way about him. He's a big spender. Likes to show off. Thinks he's a real lady's man."

"What does he do for a living?"

"Gambles a little, runs cock fights a little, deals a little. He's a construction foreman with some contracting company, but you can't live the way he does on just construction wages. I never could see why Cindy went out with him."

"It would have been the adventure of it," Jackie said. "Any other men in her life?"

"Oh, sure. You can't be as beautiful as Cindy, and a dancer, and not have men in your life," Marcella answered.

"But was Manny one of the main ones?"

"No. He didn't see her more than anyone else."

"The police report says she was found in the hotel room. If we could only find out who got the room that night. The police told us that the clerk said Cindy booked the room, but I know she didn't. She didn't use drugs and if she wanted an affair she wouldn't have done it in a place like that. Whoever gave her the drugs also booked the room, and took her there. The question is; was she just drugged when they took her there, or was she already dead? What I have to do is find out who booked the room," Jackie said.

"I do dat. Ah fine out was-da-hap."

"Can you do that?"

"Shu-ah I know pleny da kine down dere."

"Well, I got to start to get ready to go to work," Marcella said, "but if there's anything I can do, let me know, Jackie. What are you going to do?"

"I don't know. I don't know where I should be looking. I thought of going back to see Kunayoshi, but after the last time I don't think I'll learn anything there."

There was a message from Sloan on her machine when she got back to the apartment. She called him and he said, "Somebody just walked in. Are you going to be there for the next five minutes?"

"Yes."

"I'll call you back."

He called back a few minutes later and said, "Do you know anything about computers?"

"It depends on what you mean by 'know.' I operate one all the time in my business. I took a few computer courses and do a little website designing on the side for friends. I guess I could make up a simple program, but that's about it."

"That's all we need. Can you get up early in the morning?"

"I have to do it all the time if I'm going to be on line for the opening of the New York exchange."

"Good. Can you meet me at the same place at the park again and we'll talk about it. I'll bring lunch. Do you like Chinese food?"

"If you're from San Francisco, you like Chinese food."

"OK. See you in half an hour."

* * *

She sat down on the same bench they sat on before. Even at noon there were some people making their jogging way around the paths, and she thought of the saying, "Only mad dogs and Englishmen go out in the noon day sun." Behind her on the grass, and beyond that on the beach, people lay soaking up the sun. She thought that at least this time she was more appropriately dressed in shorts and blouse. In the channel in front of her sailboats were making their way out to sea getting a head start on their weekend of sailing.

He came toward her carrying two paper bags, and for some reason she felt better watching him coming toward her. He sat down setting the cartons of food and the two drinks between them. He started scraping the food out onto the plates with a set of chopsticks and said, "Well, how is your investigation going?"

"Well, Kimo is going to try and find out exactly who rented the room that Cynthia was found in, and I was going to see Kunayoshi this afternoon, and see if I could find out anything more."

"I don't think he'll tell you much."

"I don't think so either, but I hoped he might inadvertently let something drop that would help us. What did you have in mind when you called me?"

"Well, I don't know if what I am about to suggest is illegal, immoral, unethical or all three, but I hope it is all three." He was grinning like a kid about to steal a cookie from the jar. "I do know that if anyone finds out about it some people are going to be very upset."

"Oh, what's that?"

"Well, I thought we might get into Doug's computer and see what we can dig up. But I don't know very much about computers. That is a terrible thing to say in this day and age, I know. To be real honest with you the only thing I use the computer for in my office is for simple lesson preparation and things like that. So we need each other on this one. I need you to operate the computer and know where to look for what we want, and you need me to get you in since I have keys to the place and know the code that shuts off the alarm system."

"You have a key to Bautista's office?"

"I have a copy of Radford's master key that opens all the offices."

49

She smiled shaking her head a little, her hair waving with the motion. The wind was blowing her hair around her face and she ran both hands through it trying to straighten it out. "If his computer is password protected there isn't a whole lot we can do," she said. "So when do you want to do this?"

"Tomorrow would be best. That's why I called you today. Bautista never gets to the office before nine or ten on Saturday. Pastor Bell may not come in at all and the others won't be there much before nine or ten depending on what activities they have for their groups that day. I've checked the schedule and there is nothing for the youth or the children until the afternoon. Radford will be the first one there, probably about eight o'clock and the Saturday receptionist about eight-thirty."

"What time are you thinking of breaking in?" she asked.

"Is three, three-thirty too early. The earlier we get there the more time we'll have to look. I have no idea what we will find, or how long it will take."

"I'll meet you in the parking lot at three."

"It might be better if I picked you up. Since the death of your sister Doug has hired a security company to made a drive through the premises every hour or so. It would be better if there was not an unauthorized car in the lot at that hour of the morning."

"OK. You can follow me home from here to see where I live. I'll be sitting in my car in my parking stall. I don't want to stand out in the parking area, and I don't want Kimo and Marcella hearing you knocking on my door when you come to get me."

* * *

By five in the evening the bar was beginning to fill up with the Friday crowd of men who were just getting off work. The sign outside said:

NUDE DANCING
Topless and Bottomless
Continuous from 5 pm to 2 am
Happy Hour 5 pm to 8 pm.
Dancers from New York
Las Vegas and Hollywood

The last two lines were to explain that the dancers were mostly haole rather than from Korea or the Philippines.

They sat in a booth where they could watch each dancer come out of the stage door and dance the length of the bar. When they first got there, there had not been any women sitting at the bar. There were lots of waitresses. They were what a sign outside referred to as, "girls to serve you." Most of them wore see through teddies. They were on the pay role as waitresses and waited impatiently for the customers to arrive.

Soon after the dancing started there were four women sitting at the bar waiting for some man to come in and sit next to them. They all wore tight blouses some that left their shoulders and upper chest bare. Their skirts were so short that when they sat on the bar stood their thighs were exposed almost to their hips. The girls on the floor were employees, and expected the customers to touch them. If the customer bought a girl a drink she would sit down with him, and let him fondle her. Depending on how much he paid her determined whether she did something for him right there in the booth or whether they left to spend an hour together in a room in back.

The women at the bar were independents. They were there for the men who liked to sit at the bar and watch the dancers up close. The establishment didn't like them but they couldn't really keep them out because if they tried the independents might tell the liquor commission about the drug deals going down and the owners would have to pay the liquor commission people more hush money.

The bar was about four feet wide and U shaped. The dancers came out from the end of the bar dancing right in front of those sitting at the bar, stepping between the drinks, weaving back and forth, swinging a leg over a customer's head, squatting in front of them, or bending over swinging their breast just inches from their face. But it was understood that you couldn't touch the dancers. Their fingers might touch yours as you held out a five or ten to induce them to keep dancing in front of you. How long they danced in front of a customer depended on the denomination of the bill. It was then that an independent would go and sit next to the man, and with an arm around his neck and a hand gently stroking his thigh, try to get him to take her home.

Jackie sat in the corner of the booth with Kimo next to her, and Chris Wong across from her. Chris was the night clerk that had been on duty at the Nuuanu Hotel the night the police report said Cynthia died. It had not taken Kimo long to find him. He admitted that he had told the police that she had gotten the room herself because it was just easier than getting all involved with the police. He didn't know the girl who had rented the room. All he could tell them was that at about two in the morning a young, blond, haole girl had come in and paid for the room. She took the key and walked back out again without even going to her room. He had assumed that she was going out to get her customer. He had noticed her particularly because she was younger, and prettier, than most of the prostitutes that used the hotel. He didn't see her again that night, and had assumed that they had taken the back stairs to the room. It was Kimo's idea that the girl that rented the room might have been a dancer, and so they were taking Chris around to the clubs to see if he could find her.

By nine o'clock the dancers were beginning to repeat and Chris had to be at work so they called it a night. They dropped Chris at the corner of Hotel and Nuuanu and then went home. Jackie went to bed that night tired and discouraged. She was no further ahead than she had been when she arrived. Maybe the thing to do was just forget it and go home. But she couldn't do that. Finding who had killed Cynthia and Susan wouldn't bring them back, but whoever had done it should not be allowed to get away with it.

CHAPTER SEVEN

He was waiting for her when she came down from her apartment. He leaned over and pushing open the passenger side door said, "Have you had your morning coffee yet? There's some in that thermos if you want it, and that cup is clean."

"Morning coffee? I've hardly got my feet on the floor let alone had coffee. Been waiting long?"

"No. Just got here," he said waiting for her to pour her coffee. "Cream and sugar is in those packets there if you use them."

"No. Black is fine," she said taking the first sip, and he finished off what was in his cup and started out of the parking lot. At the church he parked in his assigned stall and they went inside.

It was quiet, warm, and stuffy inside with the air conditioner off. There was no sound from outside, and he said, "Whenever I'm the first one here in the morning, and it's so still and quiet it makes me think that this is what it is like inside a tomb."

He threw the switch, and there was the faint hum of the air moving through the ducts. He led the way back to Doug's office, inserted the key, threw open the door, and turning on the light said, "There it is."

She sat down at the computer and said, "I see he's one of those that leaves his computer in standby all the time, or at least he did this time. Now let's see if we can get into it. Nice up to date equipment he has here."

"Yeah, it's less than six months old. All of us got them at the same time during the summer. The old ones went to the school."

"You have the same thing?

"Exactly the same. I think I'm the only one that doesn't use it, thought,"

He was leaning over her with his left hand on the back of her chair, and his right hand on the desk. She smelled of warmth with a faint hint of some flower that he couldn't identify. He had never liked heavy perfumes. He looked from the screen to her face. She had long eyelashes, a thin, strait nose, and very clear, porcelain skin. That close to her he could see a couple of freckles on her cheek, and it surprised him a little that she had not done any makeup except for lipstick. Her eyebrows and lashes were slightly darker than her hair.

53

Leaning over like that his back began to ache which reminded him that he was fifty-five years old, old enough to be her father.

She turned her head and caught him looking at her and smiled at him, and said, "Your breathing down my neck, Dr. Sloan."

"I'm sorry," he said straightening up. "Actually, I'm not really sorry. It was just that I found your neck, and everything attached to it in both directions much more attractive than what you were showing me on the screen."

"Why, Dr. Sloan, I do believe you are flirting with me."

"First of all I'm too old to flirt, and what's more I refuse to flirt with someone that won't call me anything but 'Dr. Sloan'.—So, what have you leaned so far?"

"Well, we're in luck. He doesn't have the security enabled, just a few passwords and I can get around them."

"I thought passwords stopped you from getting into a program, or something."

"A password just lets you through the door, but there are other ways to get into the house than through the door, like through a window, or down the chimney. We'll just burn a CD of all his document files and take them with us."

He watched her not even vaguely understanding what she was doing. She brought up the folder list and started checking off items. "What is 'Agents'?" she asked.

"I have no idea unless it has something to do with the building project."

"Better take it." She named them talking to herself, but also so that he could make suggestions. "'Devotions' now we don't want that one. What about 'E-mail'? Yes we want that. 'Important notes'? We definitely want that. Don't know what it is, but we'll find out."

"If all of this is password protected, how are you going to discover the password?"

"Oh there's any number of programs that you can use to discover the password, or get around it."

"Then what protection is it?

"Oh, it's the minimal kind of protection which is fine except when determined people like you and me come along. Ah, 'Letters'. We definitely want that and 'Memos' and 'Projects'."

She went on selecting the folders she wanted, and then started the burn. "This may take a while, so let's go look at your computer."

"It's just like this one," he said going back toward his office.

She followed him in, and sat down at the desk, and then swung around to the computer that was on the table across from the desk. "When we finish the burn I'm going to put all the information from the CD into your computer and show you how you may be able to work with them. After I do you'll have to be careful working with them that you don't delete, or contaminate any of them." She said all this while booting up his computer and looking through to see what he had. "After I get through here I'm going to take the disk with me."

"I think I'll go put on a pot of coffee," he said turning away and leaving the room. When he came back she was back at Doug's computer sucking air through her clenched teeth and shaking her head. "What's wrong?"

"Everything in here is less than a three months old. It would be nice if we had some older files. I wonder were his backup disks are. If we could find those disks the files on them might not be protected. Lots of times people back things up to a disk that isn't protected because they just don't think of it, or they're in a hurry, or they want a temporary copy. Maybe he is the same way. If we could only find his backups. My guess is he isn't as careful with his copies as he is with his computer. He's probably got the disks in a drawer somewhere," she said starting to pull on the desk drawers, "But these are all locked."

"That's no problem," he said. "Momi has keys to every drawer and filing cabinet in here."

"So how is that going to help us?"

"Well I have a key that will let us into her office, I know where she hides the keys to these cabinets," he said grinning.

"Oh, how did that happen? Do you have some kind of a key finding bug?" she asked turning toward him while pushing her spread fingers up through her thick hair.

"Not exactly. And careful what you say, someone might be listening. I'll be right back. When he got back he handed her a ring of keys. "Some of those will work on these locks."

She got up taking them from him and started looking through them and trying them in the different filing cabinets. "Seriously," she said. "How did you know where these keys were?"

"Well, you've met Momi. Not an unattractive woman. About ten, maybe twelve years younger than me. She has a son in college, and a daughter just graduated from high school. Soon after my wife died I frequently found myself thrown together with her somehow. Once we were going to a meeting somewhere, and I found myself in her car. We were just starting out of the parking lot when she remembered she had forgotten a file Doug wanted for the meeting. I offered to go back and get it, and she told me where she hid the keys, and where the file was. After I got back with the folder she was obviously upset with herself for telling me where the keys were, and made me promise never to tell Doug, or anyone else, which, of course, I haven't until now."

"How noble of you, and lucky for us…Bingo. Here's a drawer full of disks and CDs."

He came and stood next to her. He could smell the fragrance from her hair. And with both of them looking at the disk label they couldn't help but brush shoulders, and hands touch as they reached for things. Her hair hung forward around her face as she looked into the files.

"How lucky can we get? He has them grouped by dates. We'll start with September to July disks and see what we can get from them," she said picking up disks and handing them to him. "Keep them in order. We don't want him to know anyone was in here."

He stood with his hands full of disks and she had a bunch of them "What are we going to do with them? We have to have them back in here reasonably soon."

"We'll have them back in an hour or less. Will just enter everything on these disks into your computer and then put them back."

He sat in the visitor's chair while she sat at his computer slipping one disk after the other copying the information. When she was done they put the disks back, and she said, "You don't by any chance have any blank disks do you?"

"No, like I told you I never use this computer except to prepare lessons and to play solitaire once in a while. But I can get some. I'm sure they have some in the supply room. What do you want them for?"

She looked at him like she couldn't believe he could be so dense. "Well if you don't know much about how to use a computer this information isn't going to do us much good here. In fact you might start messing around and erase it all. So we have to copy all the information we stole so I can take it with me and work on it on Marcella's computer."

"The one in the shop?"

"Yes."

"Why don't we just take this computer to your apartment and you can work on it anytime you want."

"Can we do that?"

"Why not. It's my computer. Well really it's the churches, but if anyone asks where it is I'll tell them I took it home for a while."

"Well let's get started," she said and started unplugging and disconnecting his computer.

They left the office, making sure everything was closed down and locked up, and went to the car, he carrying the computer, and she carrying the monitor. The sun was beginning to come up when they got to car. "Well, shall we go have some breakfast?" He asked.

"Sure as long as it has a rest room close by. I've got to get rid of all the coffee you've been giving me all morning."

They went to the Ilikai where the restaurant overlooked the marina and beach. They were among the first ones there and got a window table where they could watch the sun send shafts of light through the horizon clouds before breaking over the horizon. Even in the pleasant atmosphere of a fine restaurant they could not get away from talking about what they were doing.

"Poor Kimo," she said jokingly. "He has decided that he and Chris are to spend all day, and tomorrow if they have to, in the clubs trying to find the one that rented the room."

"Saturday and Sunday afternoons are big business in the nude bars," he said. "I have never quite been able to understand how they could combine watching a game of some kind with naked ladies dancing on a bar, but I guess for some men that's the best of both worlds."

"You know, watching those girls last night, I tried to think of Cynthia as one of them. In some ways I couldn't see her possibly doing that, and yet in other ways I could. She was always adventurous, an exhibitionist, and a tease, but she could also in some ways be very aloof, and disdainful."

"I don't know that there is necessarily any contradiction there. Her dancing may have been a form of flaunting her superiority. Like some people flaunt their money she was flaunting her perfect body and good looks. They don't mind letting you know they have the money, but they aren't going to give you any of it. She may have been doing the same thing in a way."

They finished breakfast, and went walking along the beach in front of the hotels. It was still early enough in the morning that the tourists were not out yet except for a few who, like they, were walking along the water's edge. The waves lapped soothingly on the white sand, and the trade winds brought with them the scent of the mountain flowers. But even as they walked she was eager to get to work on the information she had. She realized that her whole view of Hawaii had been, and was, tainted by the fact that she had lost two sisters there. She even thought that she could enjoy it, even like it, if trying to find her sister's killers were not the most important thing on her mind.

"You said that you never used the information you learned about people in any way. But when you learned by listening in on Don's office that some poor woman needed money, did you ever secretly get some to her?"

"The church has a system for that. We have agreements with different grocery stores and we give them a letter to the store stating that the church will reimburse the store for their groceries up to a certain amount. It is clearly understood however that they cannot buy liquor or cigarettes with the church letter."

"You haven't answered my question. What if the need isn't for groceries. Have you every helped out?"

"No."

"Then why did you decide to help me?"

"I understood a little bit how you felt. I have never understood how it is to be without groceries or to have your electricity turned off, but I do know what it is like to lose someone you love. When we first came to Hawaii we thought we had the perfect life. Not rich, but comfortable. We bought a condo and had enough to live on. We were content with what we had, and then six months after we arrived we discovered that my wife had cancer. We had health insurance but I had to go back to work to help pay the medical bills. But that's beside the point. I knew what killed my wife, and I fought it the best I could. But you didn't know who killed you sisters and I knew how it felt to want to fight the killer. That's why I left the message on your machine. If you hadn't pursued it I would have figured you didn't really care that much and you and I would not be walking along the beach right now."

"Thank you, Dr. Sloan."

"Do you think you are ever going to be able to call me 'Jim'?"

CHAPTER EIGHT

It was early Sunday afternoon when she called him and said, "Boy have I got some things to show you. Can you come over here?"

"Sure. I'm free until tonight's service."

She heard him pull into one of the visitor stalls and was standing by the door waiting for him. He walked toward her with the firm, gliding stride. He was wearing a long-sleeved white dress shirt, dark blue slacks, and black shoes, and she knew it was what he had worn in church that morning minus the tie and jacket. She pushed the screen door open and said, "You want coffee, or a coke, or anything?"

"Glass of water's fine."

"Go out on the lanai. I'll get the water."

He stopped to see where she had the computer set up on the kitchen table. "I see you bought yourself a printer," he said.

"Yep. Decided I couldn't get along without one. I was getting tired of having to run down to the Hula Shop with a disk every time I wanted to print something out."

She followed him out to the lanai with two glassed setting them on the table. "Boy do I have something to show you," she said repeating herself as she sat down. She opened a folder, took out a sheet of paper, and handed it to him.

He looked at it and said, "This is the letter from your sister. You showed it to me before."

"No I didn't. I took your advice and destroyed the one I showed you. Now where do you think I got this copy?"

"Doug's computer," he said unbelievingly.

"You know when I got the letter I thought it was strange. I mean, it was obviously printed from a computer, and Susan didn't have a computer. Not that she didn't know how to use one, but I thought, if she had access to a computer why didn't she just e-mail me?"

"So Susan didn't send you the letter. But if Doug sent you the letter how did he get all the information about Susan trying to call you, and your phone being out of order."

"The only way he could have gotten it was from Susan. All I can think of is that she turned to him for help, and he sent the letter, and then killed her."

"Why would he send a letter, and then killer her?"

"Maybe he was involved with Cynthia's death, and he had to keep her quiet."

"Yes, but then why send the letter?"

"I can't figure that one out either. Unless he is so cocky and sure of himself that he just wanted to flaunt it."

"This doesn't make any sense. But you're right, he is a cocky little son-of-a-bitch. But as cocky as he is he is not a fool. Did you find anything else that might give you a clue?"

"Not about this, but you would not believe the stuff in there. He has dirt on everyone. For you he has two dates when you rented videos for Tower Video. Both of those videos were rated NC-17."

"My, my. How disreputable. How in the world did he know that? Anything else?"

"Not about you, but would you like to know what the dark secret in Don Bjork's life is?"

"Of course I would. Why do you think I listen in on other peoples' conversations?

"Pastor Bjork was having an affair with a young lady in the church and she got pregnant. Bjork arranged and paid for the abortion, which in your church circles I assume is worse than the adultery."

"You've got to be kidding. How in the world did I miss that? I can't believe that got by me. How did you find all this out?"

"Well, I will have to admit that there was a lot of luck involved. Although he had them filed by dates, the dates in the filing cabinet were when the disk was filled. But he might have old files in the disk from six months, or even a year ago. The labels on the disk didn't tell me a whole lot. He used code words on the labels, and of course the files had code words. Since I couldn't tell from the file name what it was about I had to open every file. Do you know a Helen Abbot?"

"Yes. She's a dear old lady that volunteers around the church, and cleans the church windows."

"Her file was labeled Abbhel. It was a memo to himself which said something about her volunteering to clean the windows to pay the church back for the food she stole from the church pantry."

"That sanctimonious bastard. He steals from the church all the time, and has the gall to tell a poor old lady with nothing but social security and food stamps how to pay the church back. As administrative assistant he has a church credit card and uses it for everything from his haircuts to gas for his car."

"Susan's letter to me was 'S wants help'. That wasn't an unusual entry because apparently lots of people ask for help with buying food, or rent and so it was a common entry. But most of them were password protected. Susan's was not. Why not? Another thing that I don't understand is why when he had written a letter that was supposed to be from Susan, and mailed it, why would he keep it in the computer. That's just not smart."

"Well, what do we do next?"

"I don't know," she said putting both elbows on the table with her fingertips reaching up into her hair. "Maybe I'll see if I can get another appointment to see Doug. See if I can say some things that will jar his memory, rattle his cage."

"Why don't you come to church with me tonight?"

"Why in the world would I do that, or are you asking me out on a date."

He smiled. "Well, I wasn't thinking of it as a date, but I might play the part, and take you out for coffee afterwards. Of course you would have to sit next to me in the front row at church, and the whole congregation would be talking about it for at least a week. But actually what I was thinking is that I might get something from the comments that people would make at Tuesday's staff meeting. Incidentally, you won't get any appointments with Doug, or Don, on Monday. Except for the Pastor on duty Mondays are our day off. But come to think of it, you should come to church with me tonight. Pastor Bell always invites all the staff out to eat afterwards. You might just hear someone say something that might help us. Of course Betty Clipper will be bugging you about where did we meet, and how long have we known each other, and do you have any other men-friends. She always uses the term 'men-friends'."

"I couldn't find anything in the files about her."

"Poor Betty. She is so gross, and so desperate, and so pathetic. I can't imagine anyone wanting to go out with her let alone to bed with her. I don't like her much. She is crass, and unattractive, and dumb, but I do feel sorry for her."

"My God. The way you describe her, does anyone like her?"

"Oh, Yes! The congregation loves her. She makes no bones about wanting to get married. She cries a lot, and I think they all want to protect her as they would if she were an awkward child of their own. If she sings a solo tonight the congregation will just bring down the house with their applause. She's not bad, but they are really applauding to make her feel good, to give her something to be happy about. I will admit she is a good music director."

CHAPTER NINE

They sat crowded around the little table on the lanai of Kimo and Marcella's apartment. It was Monday, and over the weekend Kimo and Chris had finally found the girl who had reserved the room. Chris had pointed her out at a club in Pearl City the night before. She said her name was Bambi. She had long, wavy, blond hair, white-white skin and blue eyes. Kimo had put a twenty in her hand when she danced in front of him leaning over him, rolling her shoulders so that her breast swung back and forth.

"Lot more you spend night with me," he said.

She eyed him suspiciously while she did the rest of her dance until she disappeared behind the curtain and another dancer came out. He followed her from bar to bar making the same offer.

During her last dance she said, "OK"

He moved to an empty booth and a little while later she slid into the booth across from him.

"How much?" were the first words she spoke to him and he knew that she was high.

"What you want?"

"Five hundred."

He looked at her smiling for a moment. "Ain't no man ever yet pay you dat much."

"OK three hundred."

"Two," he said.

"Right now. In advance."

"Hundred now. Hundred when we be my place," he said holding out the five twenties.

She took the money, counted it carefully twice, put it in her purse. "OK Let's go." she said clutching her purse to her and standing up quickly.

He followed her out and then guided her toward his car. From the corner of his eye he saw her snort some coke as soon as she was in the car, even while he was starting the engine. She had another snort when they pulled into the parking lot.

When they got to the apartment she looked around frightened when she saw Marcella, but he gave her the other hundred and pointing to the bedroom said, "Go in bedroom."

She went in obediently, not bother to shut the door behind her, and sat down on the bed to take off her clothes. She managed to take off her blouse and undo her bra before she lay back and passed out. Marcella went in and threw a sheet over her.

She came to about ten-thirty in the morning, and they were all there waiting for her. She came groggily to the door of the bedroom and stood for a moment looking at them. "Where am I?" she asked hurrying into the bathroom.

She came out of the bathroom and went back into the bedroom shutting the door behind her.

She came out an hour later fully dressed, and made up. "What's the address here? I have to call a cab."

"I'd like to talk to you, Bambi," Jackie said getting up and going toward her. "My name is Jackie. Are you hungry?"

"Why should I talk to you?"

"Because I can help you."

"I don't need no help."

"All right then, you can help me," Jackie said.

Bambi looked at her suspiciously.

"Come on, Bambi. Let's go out here and talk."

"No! I'm getting out of here," she said.

Kimo moved to in front of the door taking his wrestler's stance blocking her way out.

"If you don't let me go I'll scream and someone will call the police."

"If the police come, Bambi, they will find the drugs you have on you, and we'll have to tell them about the room you rented at the Nuuanu Hotel," Jackie said.

She looked suddenly very frightened and said, "I ain't never been in the Nuuanu Hotel." She spoke with a soft, slow, southern-tone of voice.

"Let's go out on the Lanai and talk about it," Jackie said heading for the lanai. Bambi walked out hesitantly. She sat down at the table with Jackie on one side and Marcella on the other. Across from her Sloan started the miniature recorder in his shirt pocket.

"Bambi, do you remember a dancer named Cindy?" Jackie asked. "She was a blond about your size. She died a little over a month ago. Do you remember her?"

Bambi looked even more frightened. "Are you the police?" she asked, and then started crying.

"No! We're not with the police. Cindy was my sister," Jackie said. "Do you remember her?"

"Please. Please. Oh, I wanna go home. I just wanna go home," she wailed dropping her head to her arms on the table.

She cried for a while and then raised her head. "Please don't ask me any questions. Please, Just let me go."

"We're not going to hurt you, Bambi. We want to help you. I know you didn't have anything to do with my sister's death, but I want to find out who did."

"He'll kill me if I tell you anything."

"No he won't. We'll protect you."

"You can't protect me. Not from him."

"We can if you let us, Bambi."

Bambi silently stared at her.

"What's your real name, Bambi?" Jackie asked.

"Vanessa."

"Vanessa what?"

"Vanessa Warren."

"And where are you from, Vanessa?"

"Alabama."

"Where in Alabama?"

"Demopolis. It's bout half way between Selma and Meridian."

"Is that where you meant when you said you wanted to go home?"

Vanessa nodded slowly.

"Do you have family there?"

"Yeah. My folk are there."

"Is that what you consider your home?"

"I guess so. I left there when I was sixteen."

"How old are you now?"

"Twenty-one."

"No, Bambi is twenty-one," Jackie said. "How old is Vanessa Warren?"

"Eighteen."

"Do you want to go back Demopolis?"

"I guess so."

"If I promise to buy you a plane ticket back home will you help me?"

"I can't help you, Ma'am. I just can't."

"Vanessa, you have to help me. We have a witness who saw you rent that room that night, the very room my sister died in. If we take that witness to the police, then the police are going to want to know

64

why you rented that room. They will suspect that you are the one that was with my sister the night she died and they are going to want some answers."

"No. No. It wasn't me."

"On the other hand if you tell me what happened, and who it was that got you to rent that room, I'll buy you a plane ticket home to Demopolis."

"He'll kill me if he ever finds me. He said he would kill me if I ever told anyone. If I tell, and he finds me, He'll kill me," she said hysterically.

"We will make sure that he never finds you. We will keep you hidden until you board the plane. Now why don't you tell us what happened."

"He told me to rent the room. He said he would keep me supplied for a week if I rented the room for him."

"Who was that?"

"I can't say."

"Was it Manny?" Sloan asked.

Vanessa looked at him and started shaking with fear.

"Was it Manny Rodriguez?" Sloan asked again.

"Yes," she said quietly.

"You are saying, Vanessa, that it was Manuel Rodriguez that told you to rent the room."

"Yes. Manuel Rodriguez."

"Did he keep you supplied for a week like he promised?"

She shook her head. "He gave me a fix that night, but after that he just laughed and said if I told anyone he'd kill me."

"All right," Jackie said, "so you went into the Nuuanu hotel and rented the room. Do you remember what the room number was?"

"Two-oh-two."

"Do you remember what the date was?"

"It was Saturday night."

"Do you remember what time?"

"I don't know exactly. After two, I guess, because I was through dancing for the night. The clubs were closing."

"So it was about two o'clock Sunday morning?"

"Yeah, It was Sunday morning."

"What did you do after you rented the room for Manny?"

"I went out of the hotel to where he was waiting and gave him the key."

"Then what happened?"

"He got in his car and drove around to the back of the hotel."

"Was anyone else in the car?"

"Cindy was in there. She looked like she was asleep."

"Did he say anything when you gave him the key?"

"No. He just took it and got in his car."

"How do you know he went to the back of the Hotel?"

"I walked around there and his car was parked there. I waited there because he had promised me a fix. He and another guy were carrying Cindy up the back stairs. Then I saw him come down the back stairway."

"Was he alone?"

"Yes. I didn't see the other guy."

"Do you know the other man?"

"No. I don't think so."

"Would you recognize him if you saw him again?"

"I don't think so. I might, but it was kind of dark."

"Did Manny see you?"

"Yes. That's when he gave me the fix and told me he'd kill me if I ever told anyone I saw him that night, or that I rented the room."

"Well, your secret's safe with us, Vanessa," Marcella said. "But you should stay here until you get on that plane that's going to take you home."

"But I have to go back to my room to get my things and stuff."

"OK I'll go with you," Marcella said, "and Kimo will call his cousin at the travel place and find out about flights to Demopolis."

"Oh, there ain't no airlines go to Demopolis. I'd have to take a bus from Tuscaloosa, or Montgomery."

"Which would you rather go to?" Jackie asked.

"Are you really going to buy me a plane ticket?" She asked looking suspiciously from one to the other, her voice filled with doubt

"Yes, I really am. I said I would didn't I?" Jackie said putting a hand on her arm.

"Then I'd rather go to New Orleans. I got a brother there. I'd rather go there."

"Are you sure?"

"Yeah, I'm sure."

"OK Kimo. Get her the first available flight to New Orleans."

By the time Marcella and Vanessa got back Jackie had put everything that had been recorded into the computer and printed out a copy. Marcella had managed to keep her clean explaining that they wouldn't let her on the plane if she was high. They read what they had recorded back to her and she signed it without asking any questions.

* * *

Jackie sat sideways with one long leg bent with the foot tucked under the knee of the other leg and an arm resting on the back of the bench facing Jim Sloan. He sat with his legs crossed looking out of place on the edge of the sandy beach. He was wearing a conservative aloha shirt, long trousers and socks with leather shoes. She on the other hand looked very local with the clothes Marcella had helped her buy. She had also spent some time at the beach with Marcella so she was not as pale as she had been when she arrived a week before. She had a slight tan while at the same time her light brown-blond hair had become lighter from the sun.

On the backside of the bench the sun was sliding slowly from behind a bank of clouds into the ocean. In the other direction a few powerboats were coming in the channel and beyond that some surfers were staying out to catch the last sets before it got dark. They had taken Vanessa to the airport and watched her board the plane that would take her to LA, Dallas-Fort Worth and then to New Orleans.

"What do you think is going to happen to her?" Sloan asked.

"I don't know. Nothing good unless she can kick the habit, which isn't very likely, but she couldn't stay here. We couldn't keep her protected all the time, not with the habit she's got, and we don't really have enough to go to the police with. I'm not real sure they are anxious to solve Cynthia's or Susan's death anyway."

"I think you are absolutely right about that. I have no doubt that Manny slipped Cynthia the drugs, but I don't think Vanessa's signed statement is worth a whole lot in a court of Law. We have a suspect, but no real evidence. Do you want me to see if I can shake up some evidence?" Sloan asked.

"How are you going to do that?"

"Well we have staff meeting again tomorrow. You can bet that Betty Clipper is going to wanting to know where we went, and what we did, after we left them last night. Your being with me at church last night has them very curious. There will be questions. They know about Susan, but not about Cynthia. Telling them that you are all sisters, and that you are here trying to find out who killed your two sisters, may shake things up a little. Something like that. See if I can rattle anyone into doing, or saying something that will help us."

"What I don't understand is how, and why, Susan's body got to the church. It doesn't make sense. We know Manny was involved with Cyndi's death and because of that he and Doug may be connected to Susan's death. So it can't be either of them that would put the body there. So who did?"

"That's why I thought mentioning something in staff meeting might just shake Doug up enough that he will make a mistake."

"Sure. Go ahead. What have we got to lose?"

"Well, if Doug is the one that killed Susan, than you will have to be very careful."

"Do you think he did it?"

"I don't know. But the letter was in his computer, and he had to have had contact with Susan before she died to get your address, and all the rest of it. He claims he didn't know her, but—" he paused shaking his head a little, "and I'm absolutely sure that Manuel gave Cynthia the overdose that killed her. It may have been an accident, but he still did it.

"Now if Doug was in anyway involved, even if he only learned about it afterward, and didn't report it, then he is an accessory after the fact. My guess is that Doug is the other man Vanessa saw helping Manny. They are like brothers. If Susan had learned the truth, then she may have been killed for that. So if the killer is in the staff meeting tomorrow, and he knows that you know, you may be in real danger."

"What about you? Won't you be in danger too?"

He shrugged his shoulders. "Could be."

"Well, we've got to do something, and we'll both just have to be extra careful."

CHAPTER TEN

The room was crowded. As happened every Tuesday extra chairs were brought into Pastor Bell's office to accommodate the staff. Pastor Bell sat behind his desk with Doug Bautista on his right. It was where Doug always sat. It was an accepted place of authority. It was from there that Doug conducted the staff meeting. This morning there had been the opening announcement by Pastor Bell that Pastor Yamamoto and Pastor Bautista were both to be Senior Associate Pastors.

"Congratulations, Doug," Betty Clipper said, but aside from the there was no comments.

The meeting went on for almost an hour with the usual discussions about normal church business: the youth's camping out at Mokolele Beach, new choir robes, new insurance limitations on use of the church vans and buses, and departmental reports. Doug pronounced the meeting adjourned and Betty said, "Did you see Jacqueline yesterday, Jim?"

"Yes I did. In fact we spent almost the whole day together," Sloan said stretching his long lets out in front of him, and crossing them at the ankles which put his feet just a few inches from Doug's feet forcing Doug to slide his feet under his chair to keep from getting kicked.

"Oh, my! Oh my! Sounds interesting. Tell us about it. What did you do? Anything romantic?" she said bouncing her large frame up and down in the center of the couch, and in her excitement causing those on either side of her to bounce too. "Is anything—" She paused looking intense while waiting for an answer.

He knew that what she wanted to say was, "Is anything going on between you two?"

"Well we spent all day together yesterday—"

Betty squealed with delight,

"And we learned some very interesting things about each other."

Betty squealed again.

"You all know, don't you, that she is the sister to the woman that was found on our steps a week ago?"

Betty Clipper became suddenly very serious.

"I don't think we want to go into that anymore," Pastor Bell said running his hand nervously through his hair.

Sloan ignored him. "What most of you probably do not know is that she had another sister killed here in Honolulu a little more than a month ago. The police claimed she died of an overdose, but the thing is that Cynthia, that was her name, never used drugs. She was the one you recognized in the picture Jackie showed you," he said turning to Don Bjork. "You remember her, Don? The one you said you saw with Manny at the Fourth of July picnic."

"Oh, yeah. Her," Bjork said and, raised a hand to run a finger along the scar on the side of his freckle-covered face.

"Well, it's been established, Doug," Sloan said turning to look at Doug, "that she had been seeing your cousin, Manuel Rodriguez. She was with him and Manny brought her around to meet you at the Fourth of July picnic. Don't you remember that, Doug?"

"Manny has introduced me to so many bimbos over the years that I'm not likely to remember any one of them especially."

"But you remembered her, didn't you, Don?" Sloan said turning back to Don.

He nodded his head slowly. "I think so. Can't be absolutely sure."

"She didn't see Manny a lot, or exclusively," Sloan went on, "but she did go with him from time to time. Oh, I remember now, Doug, as a matter of fact you did meet her at the Fourth of July Picnic," Sloan said accusingly. "Don saw your cousin, Manny, introduce her to you."

Everybody was looking at Doug.

"So?" Doug said glaring back at Sloan.

"Well the police now have a signed affidavit from a girl who says your cousin, Manny, got her to rent a room for him at the Nuuanu Hotel. It was the same room in which Cynthia was found dead. But the same girl who got the room for Manny also saw Cynthia in Manny's car and later saw Manny and some other man carrying Cynthia up the back fire escape steps to the second floor of the Nuuanu hotel."

There was dead silence in the room. Heads were turning silently back and forth looking first at Doug, and then at Sloan, with confused and bewildered expressions on their faces waiting for more to be said. The only two that did not look confused were Doug and Don Bjork. Don was smiling ever so slightly, but then Don always appeared to be smiling slightly, and Doug was visibly angry.

"Are you trying to say something here, Dr. Sloan?" Doug asked speaking the name sarcastically. "I can't help what kind of trash Manny choose to hang out with and if you are trying to imply something you had better be very careful."

"Why Doug," Sloan said saccharinely, "I'm not implying anything. I'm just stating some facts. It's a fact that Manuel Rodriguez is your cousin. It's a fact that this same Manny was associating with a woman who was killed, according to the police, by an overdose of cocaine. It's a fact that this man was seen with her just before she died. It is a fact that there is a witness who can identify a second man who helped Manny carry the woman up the stairs. Those are facts.

"On the other hand, there are some things that are not facts," Sloan went on. "It is not a fact that families in Hawaii are very close, but it is accepted, it is understood, it is a 'given' if you will. And it is a fact that under the law anyone that knew about a crime and did not report it is an accessory either before, or after the fact. That's all I'm saying, Doug."

"Well, obviously I'm upset hearing things like that about any relative," Doug said getting control of himself. He stood up and gathering his papers said, "Anybody would be. I don't want to hear about it. It is none of our business."

"Oh, I'm afraid it is our business, Doug," Sloan said. "Just a week ago a woman was found dead on our steps. That woman was here trying to find out who had given the drugs that killed her sister. I think Susan got too close to the truth, and that was why she was killed. And why was she put on our steps, Doug, instead of being dumped in some sugarcane field where she wouldn't be discovered until the next harvest. By then the body would be so decomposed they wouldn't be able to identify it? It very much has something to do with us and my guess is the police are beginning to think so too. Just how it has to do with us is yet to be discovered. Aren't you curious, Doug, as to why she was put there?"

Doug stormed out of the room and Bjork was right behind him. The others stood up and crowded around Sloan. "You mean that Jacqueline had two sisters killed?" Betty asked.

There were questions from others all coming faster than he could answer them. "How did you find all this out?" Damien asked and then went on totally perplexed. "It couldn't be any of us. I mean we are all Christian. We wouldn't do anything like that."

Sloan pushed his way through them, following Bjork out, not stopping to answer any of the questions. By the time he got to his office Don and Doug were both already on their phones and he was glad he had turned on the recorders before he went into staff meeting. He picked up the earphones that went with the microphone to Doug's office.

"What do you mean he's not there," Sloan heard Doug saying. "I just talked to the office and they said he was at this site. This is Pastor Bautista, his cousin. There's been an emergency in the family. I have to get a hold of him right away—" there was a pause and Sloan wished he had bugged the telephones so he could hear what the person at the other end was saying.

"Eh, wot foe, man? Get heem!" Doug said angrily slipping into pidgin.

There was a long pause and then Doug said, "Yo in plenny pilikia, Man, bout da one wot rent da room. Meet me Likelike Drive-in."

There was another pause and Doug went back to his authoritative English. "What do you mean you can't meet me now? She signed an affidavit. You'd better meet me. I'm leaving right now and you better be there or I'm going to spill it all."

There was a pause as Doug listened, and then he said, "Oh, No! I'll tell them you just now told me about it. That you heard they had the signed statement and called me asking what you should do. That's what I'll do, man. Whose word do you think they are going to take, yours or mine? You've got a rap sheet. I don't. We've got to figure out what to do next, Man."

Doug slammed the phone down and shortly after Sloan saw him hurrying, but still swaggering, by the window on the way out.

He switched to hear what Don was saying, but there was nothing going on in there.

* * *

Radford Lee did not like bagging up the donated clothes. As custodian there were lots of jobs around the church he didn't particularly like, but this one particularly rankled him. Even cleaning the bathrooms was not as bad as going through the donation box. At least when he was cleaning the bathrooms things didn't jump out at him. In the donation box there was always a lot of the two-inch long roaches, often referred to as 'skateboards,' in among the clothes. He didn't like the way he could reach for a garment and have a roach jump on his arm, or when he was shaking it out have it land on his leg.

Another reason he didn't like it was because the things donated were representative of human nature. They were things no one wanted, but they expected others to appreciate what they threw away. Occasionally there would be something new, still in the box, but usually it was old muumuus, worn jeans, faded shirts and blouses, sweatshirts, and even socks. Sometimes the things that were thrown in there had not even been washed before they were donated. Once he had found a dirty disposable diaper in the donation box.

The donation box was somewhat hidden in an alcove across from the restrooms around the corner from the door to the church offices. It was more than five feet high with a transom type door at the top where people could drop their donations. In one side there was a door almost the size of the box itself for the removal of the clothes. It was Radford's job every two weeks to clean out the box, bag up the clothes, and take them to the volunteers' room where the Women's Ministry would sort them, clean them, and package them for distribution. Radford was careful about the way he bagged the clothes, taking each piece, and shaking it out to get rid of any cockroaches that might be in it. The women didn't like cockroaches scurrying along the tabletop when they emptied out a bag.

He took a blue flowered muumuu, gave it a quick hard shake, and stuffed it into the brown, plastic bag. He reached in for the next piece and as he did things wrapped in it fell to his feet. Even before the other things fell out he knew that it was not the usual thing found in the box. It was wrinkled, but looked almost new. It was a beautiful, emerald-green, taffeta dress, and he thought of how good his wife would look in it at the church Christmas banquet. He could get it cleaned and get a box from Macy's to put it in.

He looked at the label: "I. MAGNIN" and under it "San Francisco". He couldn't use a Macy's box and to an extent he was relieved. As nice as the dress was, and as certain as he was that he would not be able to afford anything like that for this Christmas, he didn't really like the idea of giving her something out of the donation box. He set the dress to one side, not yet quite able to stuff it into the plastic bag and reached for the things that had fallen around his feet.

He picked up the slip and a bra and was glad that the donation box was hidden from view, but still he looked over his shoulder to see if anyone was watching him. The bra and slip were half lace, and half a paisley material that matched the green of the dress. He picked up the shoes and purse, which were exactly the same color as the dress, and setting the shoes next to the dress looked into the purse. It was still full with compacts, a wallet and little cloth purses holding lipstick and other cosmetics. He opened the wallet and saw the California driver's license and even before he read the name he knew that these were *her* things.

He put the wallet back in the purse and solemnly, almost reverently, picked up the rest of the clothes. He placed the shoes on top of the purse, which was on top of the dress with the underclothes folded in it. He wondered to whom he should take it. He didn't like being the one who had found the clothes. He had to give them to someone who could take care of these matters.

Pastor Doug had left and he knew that Pastor Bell would only tell him to take it to Doug. He went into the office walking by the receptionist and secretaries hoping they would not look up and see what he was carrying. Through the rippled window he could see that Pastor Bjork had someone with him, but Doctor Sloan was sitting at his desk correcting papers. He knocked and could see Sloan get up and walk over to open the door.

"Oh, Radford. Come in," he said stepping aside to let Radford pass.

Radford sat down without being invited and held out the clothing. "I found these in the donation box. I think they're hers. Her driver's license is in the wallet."

Sloan slowly laid the things out on his desk finally opening the purse and taking out the wallet. He looked at the license and said, "You're right, Radford. You say you found all of this in the collection box."

"Yes, Sir," Radford said nodding his head emphatically so his wavy brown hair shook back and forth.

"Do you remember, Radford, if the police looked through the box last Tuesday?"

"I don't know."

"Did they ask you for the key?"

"No."

"Who else has a key?"

Radford shrugged. "Pastor Doug, of course. Probably someone from the Women's Ministry, I don't know who else."

"Do you think the police got a key from somewhere?"

"I guess they could, but they didn't get it from me."

"Either the police didn't look there or someone put these in there after they looked. Did anybody else see you find this?"

"No. I came through the office with it and you are the first one I showed it to."

"Why don't you leave them with me. Don't tell anyone you found them, or gave them to me. I want to tell Ms. Marqueoff about it before I call the police."

"Can you do that?"

"Not really. They will call it tampering with evidence but they should have looked through the box when they were first here, shouldn't they? But I think she has a right to see her sister's things before the police get them. After she has seen the clothes I'll bring them back and together we'll tell the police about how you found them."

"OK," Radford said shrugging his shoulders a little. He was glad that the responsibility was no longer his.

"Get me one of those white bags that you line the waste baskets with to put these things in, will you?"

* * *

She was waiting for him outside her door as he walked past the other apartments toward her. Kimo called to him as he passed and Sloan returned the greeting. She opened the screen door for him and followed him through the room to the lanai.

Before they could sit down he started taking the things out of the bag and laying them one by one on the glass top table. She started to cry and grabbing the dress clutched it to her. He thought that he should take it away from her so that it wouldn't get traces of her makeup or hair on it, but he let her cry into it. If they questioned her she could claim Susan was wearing it when she hugged her good-bye.

She dropped it back on top of the other things and screamed, "That Bastard! That God damned bastard."

He took her in his arms and she pounded on his chest a little while, and then clung to him sobbing. She cried for almost ten minutes and finally she pulled away from him sniffling and said, "I'm sorry."

"Don't be. You needed to cry. Are you all right now?"

She nodded, pulled out a chair, and sat down.

He sat down in the other one and said, "What I want you to do is look through her things and see if there is anything there that can give us a clue, something you might understand that the police wouldn't."

She poured the contents of the purse out on the table and he said,

"If it's plastic or smooth try to hold it by the edges so as not to leave your fingerprints on it."

She went through every little bag, and each compartment of the wallet but there was nothing there that told her anything. They put all the things back in their compartments in the purse, and then everything back in the plastic bag and he said, "Are you up to going back to work?"

"Yeah, I'm OK"

"OK good. Now you copied everything Doug had in that program is that correct?"

"As far as I know."

"Can you print it all out?"

"Sure. It will take a little time. There's an awful lot there, but, yes, we can print it all out."

"Good. Start with the most recent ones and work back for three months. Make three copies. Then you, and Kimo, and I will go over them all and see if we can get any connections."

"OK" she said shrugging her shoulder, but what do you expect to find."

"I don't know. But we know Doug was involved, or at least knows something about Cindy's death so maybe in his files we'll find some proof of his involvement."

* * *

Sloan was told that Kunayoshi was out when Sloan got back to the office and called him. He guessed that the detective just didn't want to talk to him, which was all right with Sloan. It was not that he didn't want to give the clothes to Kunayoshi, but he suspected that the detective did not think Sloan had anything of value and considered anything that Sloan might do as interfering. It was late in the afternoon when Kunayoshi called back.

"Thank you for calling, Mr. Kunayoshi, I have something here that I think you'll be interested in. It appears to be the victim's clothes. Apparently your men didn't search as thoroughly as they should have. Anyway, I have them here in my office if you want them."

He knew Kunayoshi would be angry at the comment about his men not searching very well.

"Did anyone touch anything?"

"Of course we touched them. How do you think they got from

where they were found to my office?"

"I'll send a man around to get them."

"Why don't you come yourself? I have something else here that has to do with the Cynthia Harcourt case that I think you might find interesting."

"Look, Sloan—"

"Doctor Sloan to you, Mr. Kunayoshi," Sloan said interrupting him.

"Stay out of police business. You'll only confuse things and get yourself in trouble."

"I don't know how I can get in trouble when I'm only being helpful. After all, we found the clothes when you're people couldn't. I haven't told anyone that yet, but I think the news media would be interested to know how efficient your people are. After the media is finished the Feds might be interested. I don't know of any reason why they would be interested but you never know with the Feds."

"I'm warning you, Sloan," Kunayoshi said and hung up the phone.

Kunayoshi was there in fifteen minutes. He sat in the chair at the side of the desk hunched forward like a frog about to spring, his glasses magnifying his eyes. Radford sat in a chair next to Sloan. Sloan handed Kunayoshi the plastic bag and Kunayoshi emptied the contents out on the desk. He put on a pair of plastic gloves before picked up each item and even then he was very careful to hold them between his thumb and forefinger. When it came to handling the wallet he held it by the edges. When he was through looking through it all he dropped everything back into the bag.

He tied the bag shut and said, "What's the other thing you think I'll be interested in?"

Sloan handed him an envelope with a copy of Vanessa's statement. He read it and said, "This is just a copy."

"That's right," Sloan said spreading his hands and raising an eyebrow apologetically. "I'm afraid that's all I have."

"I can't do anything with a copy. Where is the original?

"Surely you must be able to do something with a copy. After all, if there is a copy there has to be an original somewhere. But the copy's all I have."

Kunayoshi slapped the folded piece of paper against a hand and said, "So where is this Vanessa Warren?"

"I don't know where she is, but I do know that Doug Bautista met Manny Rodriguez at the Likelike Drive-in around noon today. I don't think they are still there. But with that statement from Miss Warren it seems to me that they should both at least be talked to about the first sister's death."

"I told you before, and I'm telling you again, Sloan, stay out of our business. You amateurs just—" he paused remembering he was in a church building and looked for another word, "mess things up."

"Just trying to be helpful," Sloan said shrugging his shoulder.

"Yeah, well, don't be," Kunayoshi said and stalked out.

CHAPTER ELEVEN

It had been a week since Sloan had given Kunayoshi Susan's clothes and Vanessa Warren's statement. The police had never admitted it, but it seemed that the police had looked everywhere for the clothes except in the donation box. They had looked in the dumpsters, in every nook and cranny around the church, in the storm drains, in the bushes, in the trashcans, and behind the stools in the rest rooms, and even in the toilet tanks, but not in the donation box. They claimed that someone had to have put Susan's things in there after they searched the box. But neither Radford, nor anyone else remembers them asking for a key to open the box, and they couldn't have pulled the contents out through the top door. What had happened was that one officer had gone to find a key to the donation box and been distracted to something else and the box had been overlooked.

There had been another flurry of the police questioning people at the church but nothing had changed in the three weeks since the body had been found. Manny was still going about his business and that morning Doug had again presided over the staff meeting. The only thing of interest in the staff meeting that morning had been Doug's announcement that the Building Committee had met again over the weekend and they had gotten down to the last three bidders. The bids were for making the parking lot under the school building into classrooms.

Doug looked and sounded importantly superior when he said, "The committee still has a little more work to do but the contract will probably be awarded next week."

It was not a really large project but it would give the school four more large rooms plus office space and toilets. The reason everyone, and his brother, bid on it was because there was a good possibility that if the contractor did a good job on the class rooms, he would be in a very good position to get the contract for the new church which was a twenty million dollar project. Doug managed to mention the church project whenever he had talked about the classroom project with the various bidders.

"Who are the three finalists?" Don Bjork asked running a finger along the scar on his cheek.

Doug tried to sound very important when he said, "Well, we're not divulging that information yet."

"In other words," Sloan said picking up on what Bjork had asked, "There is a good possibility that the one who gets the contract will tell the media and everyone will know about it before the church ministry leaders do?"

"What about that, Doug," Pastor Bell said. "Dr. Sloan has a point there. I think the people in this room should know about it before anyone else."

"I still would prefer, Sir, not to tell anyone right at this time. We can let the staff know when we have made our selection just before the official announcement is made next week. There are still some little details that have to be worked out. And I just prefer not to divulge the information until the final papers have been signed. This kind of information tends to leak out before it should and can sometimes complicate matters."

"Do all the members of the building committee know about it?" Sloan asked.

"Of course."

"In other words, you feel this is so confidential that anyone on a committee, who is a member of the church, who may very well talk about it with someone where he works, who can then mention it to someone else, can know about it, but the pastoral staff can't?" Sloan asked sarcastically.

Bell didn't like these power struggles. "All right, let's get on with the meeting. Even I don't know for sure who will get the contract. When the time comes we'll all know. In the meantime let's get on with it, shall we?"

From the way Pastor Bell said that, Sloan knew that the committee had recommended three thinking they were leaving the final decision up to Pastor Bell. It was the way Doug controlled things. Of the thirty or so companies that submitted bids there were those that were obviously too high, others that were just not competent to do the job. Of the dozen or so that were left the committee had chosen three that for all practical purposes were about equal.

Doug had told the committee that Pastor Bell really should have the final decision. Then he would turn around and tell Pastor Bell that the Committee was strongly recommending one of them, the one Doug had settled with. When the final decision was made Pastor Bell would choose the one Doug recommended, the one that had promised Doug the most in kickback if they got the contract.

Sloan had just gotten back to his office after the staff meeting ended when he saw Doug, briefcase in hand, swaggering down the hall on his way out. He opened his door and stuck his head out in time to hear Doug telling Momi that he would be gone for the day, and would call back from time to time for any messages. Sloan guessed that Doug was probably on his way to talk to those who were still in the running to get the job. He would not overtly suggest they give him anything, but he would explain to them that the final decision had not yet been made, but they were among the final three. He would leave them to think about what they could do to assure they got the contract. They would all know that the surest way to get the contract was to pay Doug something. It would assure they got it. The big question they would have to decide was how little they would have to give him. They would have to factor into that thinking of who they thought the other two finalists might be and what they might be willing to pay.

Sloan pulled back into his own office closing the door behind him and turned on the recorders just in case something interesting should be said in one of the offices. He worked for a while on a couple lesson plans and left about noon to meet Jackie for lunch. He sat with her and Kimo on her lanai with the lunch dishes cleared away. They were all a little discouraged. They seemed to be getting nowhere. During the past week they had all gone over the printouts of Doug's letters and memos, but had not found anything.

"You know, Jim," Jackie said, "it's just like you said. Kunayoshi isn't doing a thing about trying to solve this case. He doesn't care about it. You and I aren't from here so he doesn't care if he solves the case or not. If I go back to the mainland tomorrow that will be the end of it."

Neither of the men answered her at first and then Kimo said very excitedly which made his pidgin that much harder to understand, "Das it, Man! It not dat they no have one make dem ta-do sompin, eet dat they have da kine tell dem not ta-do sompin. Da not ta-do moe impodand dan da ta-do."

"What did he say?" Jackie asked

"He said that it is not that they don't have someone making them do something, but that there is someone pressuring them not to do something. The person, or thing telling them not do anything is more important than the pressure to do something."

"So the question is, who stands to gain by their not

81

investigating?" Jackie asked thinking out loud.

"Manny and Doug, of course. They don't want to be accused of a crime, but I can't think of anyone else. If I could we'd have something more to work on," Sloan said shaking his head.

"One dat don wan sompin happen wit investigatin, mebe da one dat wan sompin hoppen some nuddah place."

"What is he saying?" Jackie asked embarrassed that she didn't understand him again.

"I think you've got something, Kimo," Sloan said. "What Kimo is saying," he said turning to Jackie, "is that Kunayoshi and his gang are holding back because someone either wants something to happen, or something not to happen before the police do anything. Someone is telling Kunayoshi to hold off. We know that Doug at least knows about Cynthia's death, but as far as I can tell he's never been questioned about it. Whenever the police go into talk to him they ask the same questions they've asked before about his finding Susan, but they never talk about Cynthia. And they don't talk about Susan very long. They are almost immediately talking story about when they were kids in Kalihi."

"Is old Haole way. If-en you know important person nothing happen to you. Never no find out what happen, always first find out who know who. Now-a-day is more bettah go after new people. Them that just now come from Philippine, and Korea, and Viet Nam. All what no got family here. Throw them in jail. They no got family give pilikia."

"The question is, why aren't they going after Doug?" Jackie said frowning and then added, "aside from the fact that he has lots of family and all that, unless he has something on them. He has something on just about everybody. I still think we should have given Doug's internal memo about Manny to Kunayoshi. At least it would have shown that Doug knew about it and that he was there."

"We've been over this Jackie. You yourself said that it would just have been an admission that we invaded his computer. As you said before, they would need a search warrant to go into his computer, and before they could get there he could erase the file. They could even claim we put it in there."

"I know. I know. I'm just getting antsy. Let's look over the papers again, and see if we can find anything."

"Jackie, we've done that, I don't know how many times."

"I know, but let's do it again," she said getting up, and going to get the stack of papers. She divided the papers between Sloan and herself. They each had a stack that was more than an inch high. The pages were getting a little tattered around the edges. They started looking through the papers again, and Kimo went next door and brought back the hat he was making out of Lau hala. He sat down on the floor. It was hard to believe how fast those thick, stubby fingers could move weaving the fronds.

They turned the pages over, one at a time, for about fifteen minutes, and Jackie suddenly and excitedly said, "Kimo's right. It's not that Doug has something on someone, but that he has something they want - the contract. Looking at all these letters and memos it came to me. He controls who gets the contract.

Sloan stared at her for a moment and said, "You may have something there."

"Doug didn't tell you who the final bidders were?"

"No. He's probably negotiating his kick-back."

"Well we know who submitted bids because we have Doug's letter acknowledging that the bid was received. And there have been some of them that have already been notified that their bid was rejected. So start through them again and look for the letters acknowledging that the bids have been received. Unfortunately they are filed by the contractor's name so they won't be in clusters..." she paused for a moment and pushing the hair from her face said, "better yet lets go to the computer. They are filed by name, but the descriptions are all the same. I remember them 'receipt of bid' and 'notice of bid rejected' or something like that."

It didn't take them long on the computer. When they were through there were nine companies that had submitted bids that had not received a rejection notice. The Committee's meeting Saturday morning had been to choose three from among those nine. They took the names back and sat down with Kimo to find out who was related to whom. What they were looking for was some important person in the company that might be related to Doug. Kimo knew a lot about some of them and very little about others. It was about four in the afternoon and they were on their sixth name when Kimo said, "He brother big drug head."

"A dealer?"

"No. No. He head drug man with police."

"Head of Narcotics?"

"Yeah."

"That's our connection," Sloan said. "The reason the police haven't gone after Doug is because Japac Construction and

Development wants the contract. The president of Japac construction is brother to the head of narcotics, and he has talked to the head of homicide who has told Kunayoshi to hold off. They are not going to do anything about Susan's and Cynthia's death until they have the contract. Their investigation started pointing toward Doug, and they pulled back. I can almost guarantee that Japac will get the contract, not only for the classroom building, but for the new church. Not only do they want something Doug has, but they also have something hanging over his head."

"What are we going to do about it?"

"We're going to lie like hell. What's the name of the President of Japac?" Sloan asked taking the printout from Kimo to see who it was addressed to.

"Woodrow Haramoto."

They found the Japac number and gathered around the phone in the bedroom with the notes they had made. They turned on the speakerphone and punched in the number. "Japac Construction and Development," a voice said sweetly.

"This is Pastor Bell's secretary at the First Aloha Christian Tabernacle. May I have Mr. Haramoto's office please," Jackie said

"One moment please," the voice said and there was a slighting clicking and ringing. Jackie sat tapping her long, polished fingernails nervously on the table. Sloan reached over and touched her hand, and she pulled her hand back as another voice said, "Mr. Haramoto's office."

"This is Pastor Bell's secretary. Is Pastor Bautista there?"

"No he isn't. He was here earlier, but he left soon after he and Mr. Haramoto came back from lunch."

"Is Mr. Haramoto there? Pastor Bell would like to talk to him if he's free to talk."

"One moment please."

The phone went quiet for a moment and then a voice said, "Haramoto."

"Thank you Mr. Haramoto. One moment please, Mr. Haramoto. Pastor Bell is waiting to talk to you."

Jackie pressed the hold button and then released it and Sloan Said, "Mr. Haramoto. Good to talk to you again. I understand Pastor Bautista met with you earlier today."

"Yes. We had lunch together. I understand you will be awarding the contract next week," Haramoto said.

"Yes, that's what I'm calling you about. I was hoping Pastor

Bautista could stop by and see you again today, but something has come up so I thought I'd call you myself. I just wanted to let you know myself that we are going to award the contract to someone else."

There was a long silence and then Haramoto said, "Did Pastor Bautista know this when we met for lunch today?"

"No he did not know of it then. He knows of it now, of course. Pastor Bautista and I met with the Committee again this afternoon when the decision was made. You will of course be getting an official letter, but I wanted to let you know personally."

"I see. Is there any possibility that you might reconsider?"

"I don't think so. The Committee has made its decision and I concur with them. You might be glad to know, however, that Pastor Bautista insisted on you being the contractor right up to the last vote. He was very adamant about it, but I'm afraid he failed to sway the committee. I want to thank you for submitting a bid, and maybe we can do business in the future. But as I said, I wanted to tell you personally so you wouldn't be surprised when the letter arrived," Sloan said as they all held their breath.

"Thank you, Pastor Bell. Good-bye." Haramoto said and hung up abruptly.

"Now what do we do?" Jackie asked.

"Just sit back and see what happens, and hope like hell that Doug doesn't call Haramoto about something. I think Haramoto is angry enough that he won't call Doug. Just hope nobody calls anybody. We will know very shortly if our guess was right. If we are wrong they will all be wondering what happened and thinking the other person is lying. If they start investigating, I mean really investigating Doug, then maybe we should give Kunayoshi a call suggesting that if he looks in Doug's computer he would find memo's connecting Doug with Manny and Cynthia's death. But we can't do that until we know for sure that they are really going after Manny and Doug."

CHAPTER TWELVE

It was the day before Thanksgiving and there was about the office the excitement normal for the day before Thanksgiving. There would be the regular Wednesday night service, but everyone's thoughts were toward the next day. There was always Thanksgiving service with a special musical production. Although the choir had been practicing for weeks, Betty Clipper was running around, not really getting anything done, but worrying about the next day's special music. After the Thanksgiving service Pastor Bell would, as he always did, take all the pastors and their wives to the Summit for the Thanksgiving buffet dinner.

The two detectives arrived in the middle of the morning. They were very polite, almost friendly, when they asked Pastor Bautista if he could accompany them to the station. They made it sound as though he were one of them who had special information. He left, walking with a swagger, joking with them as they headed toward their cars. He was obviously not someone that was under suspicion. They said that he was perfectly free to take his car but he might have problems finding a parking place and they would certainly have someone give him a ride back as soon as they were finished talking to him.

It was about three thirty-thirty when Sloan got a call from Jackie. "Has Kunayoshi called you?" Jackie asked.

"No. Why?"

"He called me a little while ago and said he wanted to see both you and me right away. I guess he expected me to do his dirty work for him and tell you about it."

"I'll pick you up," He said. He was just starting out of his office when Doug returned definitely not as cocky as he had been when he left. He called to Momi as he went into his office, and she got up from her desk in the office across from his and followed him into his office. Sloan hurried back into his office and had his earphones on just in time to hear Momi close the door behind her.

"Momi, the police have taken my cousin Manny in for questioning in connection with some girl that died of an overdose. They think he had something to do with it and because Manny and I are such close family they also think I knew something about it. They also hinted that they think I know something about the way that other woman died just because I found her."

"Oh, no, Pastor Doug. Not you."

"They are still holding Manny and I don't know if they are thinking of arresting me or not, but I have to get things in order here."

"Is there anything I can do?"

"Now you know, Momi, that lots of people confide in me. I don't know if the police are going to get a search warrant that will let them look through my files or not. They would never find anything there, but I can't let them see the reports I have kept on people who have confided in me about their problems. Fortunately tomorrow is Thanksgiving and they won't be able to get any search warrants before Friday. But I can't let them snoop into the confidential files of people in this church who have confided in me," he said repeating himself.

"No. Of course not. Isn't that under some kind of immunity or something? I mean they can't make a Pastor or a priest tell what people tell them, can they?"

"Yes, but the police don't always recognize that. I'm going to delete any sensitive files from my computer. What I want you to do is take all these back-up disks and CDs home with you and don't tell anyone you have them. Maybe even give them to someone else to keep for you so that if anyone asks you if you have any files, or anything you can honestly say you don't."

"I'll be praying for you, Pastor Doug," she said starting to put all the disks into a box.

"Thank you, Momi. I don't know what I'd do without you," he said starting to delete files from his computer.

* * *

Kunayoshi was positioned, as he always seemed to be when they arrived at his office, with his chair pushed a little back from his desk. He sat forward in his chair, his hands on his knees, his elbows clamped against his side. His head was back looking up through the thick glasses. Today he resembled a frog about to dart a tongue out to catch an insect.

He did not greet them in any way, or even ask them to sit down, but opened with, "I told you before, Ms. Marqueoff, not to go poking into things. I have a good notion to ask the prosecutor's office to charge you with obstruction of justice."

87

"Obstruction of justice," Sloan exploded leaning over the desk, "what the hell you talking about?"

"Vanessa Warren. She was a material witness and now she's gone."

"You didn't have her as a witness at all until we found her for you. We got a signed statement for you. We didn't obstruct, we helped," Jackie said bristling.

"Where is she now?"

"I have no idea. Can we go now?"

"No."

"Why not? We came in voluntarily and you have been nothing but rude to me since we first met. You want to talk to me, get a subpoena," she said starting to turn away to leave.

"There is also the matter of the clothing."

"What clothing?"

"The victim's clothing. Instead of calling the police everybody under the sun saw it, and handled it before we were called."

"Oh, come off it, Mr. Kunayoshi. Your people didn't even find the clothing."

"It was put in that box after we made our search."

"What did you do, get a locksmith to open the lock for you instead of asking the janitor for the key?" Sloan said sarcastically.

"And then there's the matter of the letter."

"What letter?" Jackie asked.

"The letter you got from your sister. The one you showed to Pastor Bjork. The one she wrote just before she died? The one where she said she knew who your other sister's killer was."

Sloan and Jackie looked at each other and then Jackie said, "Pastor Bjork told you about that letter?" she said genuinely surprised.

"Yes he did."

"He shouldn't have done that. I thought my conversation with him was confidential. I can't believe Pastor Bjork told you about that letter."

"I'd like to see that letter," Kunayoshi said.

"I don't think she's under any obligation to show you that letter," Sloan said, "and Pastor Bjork was out of line mentioning it to you. Information given to a member of the clergy in the confessional, or in counseling is privileged. And a letter between two people is private, especially when it was as vague as that letter was."

"Did you see the letter?'

"No," Sloan lied, "but I was told about it. And I still don't think she is under any obligation to show it to you."

"We are dealing with a capital crime here and it is not as though a person's rights are being jeopardized."

"I don't know about that, Kunayoshi," Jackie said, "but I do know you are trying to play games with us. Whoever told you about any letter is just hearsay, isn't it? So why are you bugging me about it?"

They started to leave again, and Kunayoshi said, "Ms. Marqueoff, don't you want to help us find your sister's killer?"

"I don't think that letter is going to be of any help to you. Actually I've lost the letter, but I can tell exactly what it said. This is it exactly. I read it so often I memorized it. 'Dear Jackie, I think I've found him, and I think he knows who I am, and why I'm here. I know you said we were not to put anything in writing, but I tried calling you several times, and got a message that your number was no longer in service. I am desperate. I think he is trying to kill me. Please call me. Susan.' That's all there was to the letter, Detective. Now if you'll excuse me, we're leaving."

"Did she ever mention who she thought the killer was?" Kunayoshi asked.

"No."

"Why didn't you want anything in writing?" Kunayoshi tried to ask, but they were out the door.

They didn't say anything until they were in the car. "You didn't tell Don about the letter, did you?" Sloan asked.

"Absolutely not. That's why I kept repeating his name expecting that somewhere along the way he would correct me and say that it was Doug that mentioned it. After all, you said Doug was there all day."

"I don't understand it. Do you think Doug is the one that told him about it and he mistakenly said Bjork, and then let you go on, and from what you said thought that Bjork knew about it too?"

"I don't know. I just don't know. But I do know that I never told Pastor Bjork about it."

They were quiet the rest of the way to her apartment and when they were inside she said, "I just can't figure it out. We find the letter in Doug's computer, but Kunayoshi says Bjork knows about it. How many people in that office have computers?"

"Everyone, I guess. There's four in the secretary's office, Pastor Bell's secretary has one, the one in Doug's office, of course, Momi, and then Don Bjork, Damien Pasqual and Betty Clipper all have personal ones at home in addition to the ones at church. That's not counting the ones in the accounting office which as I understand it is a whole different system. When the church was getting new computers for everyone on the staff, Doug tried to talk everyone into getting one for themselves. He claimed that because they were buying so many of them they would get a very good price, and I guess they did. I know there was a slew of computers that came in. We all got a new one. In addition there were new ones for all the school offices. I'm sure Doug got a commission on every one the church bought.

"Than anyone of them could have gotten into Doug's computer and seen that letter just like we did if they knew the password."

"Or they could also have put the letter in there. They could have gone in there sometime when no one was around, or when Doug stepped out for a few minutes to go to the restroom, or to Pastor Bell's office, and written the letter, or brought it in on a disk."

"What your saying is that maybe Doug didn't write the letter. Doesn't even know it's in his computer."

"That's possible, isn't it?"

"Of course it's possible, but who?"

"That's our big question. But it has to be someone in the church. Everyone is saying they never saw Susan before, but someone did. We have jumped to the conclusion that it has been Doug all along. When did you get the letter?"

"Monday morning. I tried calling her several times that day and night, and when I couldn't get a hold of her I caught the plane out here Tuesday."

"You got the letter Monday. When was it mailed?"

"She didn't put a date on her letter, and I didn't really look at the postmark. The latest it could have been mailed for me to get it on Monday would have been Friday, but that would be with every connection going just right through the post office."

He nodded. The letter could have been mailed Friday or Saturday, and you wouldn't have gotten it till Monday. In fact it could have been mailed at the airport Sunday morning, and if you were very, very lucky you might have gotten it Monday, but that is very unlikely. I don't see that there is anything we can learn from when you received it because when it was mailed is strictly speculation. Now let's go over the letter line by line. What's the first sentence?"

"I think I've found him, and I think he knows who I am and why I'm here."

"Him. Who is Him?" he asked reaching for a pad of paper and taking a pen out of his pocket. "We have to put down everyone it could possibly be." He said the names as he wrote them on the pad. "Manny, Doug, and then everyone at the church, Pastor Bell, Don Bjork, Damien Pasqual, Me," he said raising an eyebrow, and writing his own name, "and Radford Lee. Those are the men that have general access to the offices. Oh, and old Herbert Yamamoto. Do we want to list Betty Clipper and all the secretaries?"

"I don't know," she said. "Since you ask I assume you do not consider any of them suspects."

"Do you?"

"No. After all, Susan said 'him' in her letter. Incidentally, are the secretaries assigned to anyone, or is it a secretarial pool?"

"Martha Bellows is Pastor Bell's secretary, and Momi is Doug's secretary. The rest of us just put our stuff in the 'out' box, and it is collected twice a day and Ann assigns someone to do it."

"Maybe put Momi on the list. From what you've said I gather she and Doug are kind of close."

He tore out another sheet of paper and drew lines the length of it. At the top of the page between the lines he wrote, "Motive," "Opportunity," "Ability," "No Alibi," and then started writing the people's names down the left hand side. He looked at the grid with the categories across the top and the names down the left side and said, "This doesn't mean too much yet because we don't have any idea of who had an alibi for the time Susan was killed except for Radford. I don't have an alibi for that night. I was home alone. We'll just keep this and check off what we learn as we go along," he said slipping the page under some others on the pad. "I'll have to see if I can find out who was where that night. Okay. What's the rest of that sentence."

"I think he knows who I am, and why I'm here."

"Well, we know who she was, and why she was here. What's the next sentence?"

"I know you said we were not to put anything in writing."

"Why was that?"

"A paper trail is actually very hard to get rid of. You have to shred it, or burn it. I don't have a shredder, and I don't like playing with fire. Considering what she was doing I just thought it wiser, especially if she wrote something and the wrong person over here got it before she mailed it."

"That's sensible. What's next?"

"I tried calling you several times and got a message that your number was no longer in service."

"You've already told me what happened there, but let's go over it again."

"I had just moved. There was a mix up with the phone company. They stopped service at the old place before they started it at the new place."

"Wouldn't they just give the caller the new number?"

"My number is unlisted."

"When exactly did all this happen? When did the service to the old number stop?"

"It must have been Wednesday. It might have been Tuesday. I was busy with last minute packing and didn't make any calls so I didn't know it was off." Sloan was making notes as she talked. "The movers were there Thursday. I tried calling Susie Thursday evening from the new place and discovered that I didn't have service yet."

"Did you try calling her Friday?"

"Oh, Yes! Friday, Saturday, Sunday, and I got the letter Monday. That's why I was so upset. Not only could I not get a hold of her, but her answering machine was not on for me to leave a message."

"Did she have a cell phone you could have tried?"

"It's hard to believe in this day and age, but she didn't have a cell phone, or if she did she never gave me the number."

"So where was she that weekend?" he asked more to himself than to her. "Let's just agree she mailed the letter Friday. That's Friday, Saturday, Sunday and Monday that can't be accounted for. You were continually calling her, so if she were home she should have picked up her phone. Where was she during that time?"

"That's what I want to know?"

"When was the last time you talked with Susan?"

"On Tuesday the week before I came here. I told her about moving. I was going to give her the new number. The telephone company had told me what it would be and I had written it down, but I didn't have it with me, so I told her I'd call her again on Thursday and give it to her."

"So it was a whole week without talking to her."

"How did she sound? What did she say when you talked to her Tuesday?"

"Well she hadn't sounded real up ever since she came back to Hawaii and you can understand why. I haven't been real up myself. But she didn't sound any different than usual."

"Did she say anything?"

"She said she thought she was close; real close, but she's said things like that before."

"Whoever wrote that letter had to have gained her confidence. If she was getting close to Manny and had made a connection between Manny and Doug, then she had to have talked to someone else," Sloan said.

"But she didn't have Kimo to tell her the things he's told us about Manny and Doug."

"Susan probably went right to other dancers," Sloan said. "The other dancers would have known about Manny. Did she ever mention other dancers, or the clubs?"

"She just mentioned that she had talked to people who were Cindy's friends, but she didn't really mention any names." She paused for a moment and said, "How did she get around?"

"What do you mean?"

"When I got here I took a taxi. Then Kimo drove me around a couple of days and then I rented a car."

She got up and started out of the apartment, and he followed her. She walked into Kimo's apartment without even knocking. He was sitting on the floor surrounded by Lau leaves. "Kimo, did Susan have a car?"

"Yeah. She have one blue Camry."

"Where did she park it?"

"Same like you."

"In the stall that goes with the apartment?"

He nodded.

"What kind of car did Cindy have?"

"She no have car. When she wanna shop she go with my sistah when she go to get da kine groceries."

"What about getting to work."

"She all time walk, or take bus. Work club close by. She work all clubs on Keeaumoku, then Kona, like that. If anyone give her pilikia then I drive her, or she barrow car. You fine someting?"

"We don't know. But if we can find where Susan's car is that might tell us something."

"She rent from AVIS."

"How do you know?"

"I see the sticker on the bumper."

"Thank you Kimo."

* * *

The girl in the Waikiki AVIS office didn't want to give them information but when Sloan said, "Do you remember a couple of weeks back when a body was found on the church steps?"

"Yes."

"Well that was this woman's sister. The girls name was Susan Harcourt. She rented a blue Camry from you people. All we want is the license number to help the police find the car and maybe even the killer."

"I'm sorry," the clerk said looking quickly at Jackie, "Sorry about your sister," she said and looked away awkwardly and punched some keys on the computer. "The license number is BYN 575."

"Anything else you can tell us?" Sloan asked writing down the number.

"She rented it first for a week. Then wanted it for another week, and last time rented it for month. It's due back in ten days."

"Thank you. Thank you very much."

By the time they got out of the rental agency it was too late to go to see Kunayoshi. Their hope was that if they could find the car they would have some clue as to where Susan had been just before she was killed. They drove around for a while along streets that didn't have parking restrictions hoping they might just see the car.

They went back to her apartment working on the list of what they knew, and didn't know, and when they had everything written down they admitted they didn't know very much. Sloan left when he had to get back to the church for the Wednesday night service.

It was about half an hour after Sloan left that the phone rang. Jackie thought for some reason it was Sloan and so didn't bother to let the answering machine screen it but answered it.

"Ms. Marqueoff?"

"Yes."

"This is Radford Lee, the custodian at the church. I found something I thought might belong to your sister."

"How did you get my number?"

"In Doctor Sloan's phone-file. I know you've been seeing him quite a bit so I figured he'd have your number."

"I see. You're the one that found her clothes, aren't you?"

"Yes, Ma'am."

She couldn't remember when she had heard someone use the expression "ma'am" last, and to hear someone address her that way made her feel old. "What did you find, Mr. Lee?"

"A locket. It has a picture in it. I don't know if it is your sister's, or not. I found it this afternoon in the parking lot when I was sweeping. I tried to call you then but there was no answer."

"Why didn't you leave a message?"

"I don't like answering machines."

"I understand. When can I meet you?"

"Right now if you want. The service is going on, but you could come by, and I can show you where I found it."

"OK I'll be right over. Where shall I meet you?"

"I'll be waiting for you in the parking lot."

He motioned her into a parking stall and went and opened the door for her. She got out and he handed her the locket. She walked over to a light in the parking area under the condominium, and opened the locket. "It's Susan's," she said. "That's a picture of her mother and father. They died when she was five."

"I thought if it was hers you might like to have it."

"Thank you. Where did you find it?"

He led the way between the parked cars to the area under the building reserved for the pastors. "It was right over here under the edge of this stopper. I saw it when I was sweeping up. I don't sweep regularly, just when it looks like it needs it with leaves and such," he said explaining why he hadn't found it earlier.

"Are these lights on all the time at night?" she asked.

"No. They're on a timer. The big lights all go off at eleven. The only ones left on are those three bulbs down the middle there," he said.

"It wouldn't take much for someone to unscrew them. A tall man could reach them very easily, couldn't they?"

"Yes, Ma'am."

"What do you think happened that night?"

"I don't know. I'm not very good at these kinds of things," he said hesitantly.

"What kind of things is that?"

"Figuring out how things happened."

"But you have some ideas. We all have ideas. You found my sisters clothes and when you found them you wondered. You thought about it, wondered how the clothes got to be there. Now you've found this locket and when you found it you began to wonder. You thought it was my sisters and you started to think about it. A person can't help but think about it. So all I'm asking is what do you think?"

95

He paused for a while staring at her in the harsh lights of the parking lot and finally said, "I think he pulled in here and parked somewhere around here where I found the locket. Like you say, he reached up and unscrewed the three bulbs and then he went into the church and turned off the lights there; in the foyer, and the flood lights in front. He turned off the lights in the offices and then came back, and carried the body to the steps, and then took the clothes and threw them in the donation box. Or maybe he undressed her here," he said shrugging his shoulders.

"Would someone have seen him?"

"I came back a few nights later and went around and turned off all the light just as I described, and it is very dark in here."

"You really have been thinking about it a lot, haven't you?"

"I guess so, Ma'am. It is awfully dark in here with all the lights off. Come—" he said leading the way from the parking area under the building.

They stood on the edge of the playground area, which was also filled with parked cars. He waved his hand at the surrounding buildings when he said, "The playground is surrounded on three sides by the back sides, the dark sides, of the buildings. When the church is dark, and these lights are off," he said waving toward the florescent lights back where they had been, "and these lights in the playground are off, what little light there is comes from that row of small windows," he said pointing to the high-rise across the street. "I think those are all bathroom windows. Not much light from them even if they were all on. The night I was here there were only three of them on. Not much light from there. You can see right now there's not many of them on. This fourth side is an empty lot, and it has a fence around the whole thing so there's not likely to be anyone in there. At the front of the church it's not as dark because of the street light at the corner, but the steps are pretty much in the dark because of the hedge, and the pine tree that blocks out the street light."

"Do you have an idea who it was?"

"We all have our favorite suspects, don't we? Of course the police have already checked my alibi. I was in class from seven till nine. After class I picked up a pizza at Pizza Hut on University and took it home. I got home with the pizza about ten. My wife and her brother, who is staying with us, know I was home all night."

"Who is your favorite suspect?"

"A pastor."

"Which one?"

"One tall enough to unscrew those bulbs. I've got to go now."

"Thank you for the locket. Are you going to tell the police you found it and gave it to me?"

"What for? They wouldn't do anything with it but keep it locked up somewhere until one of them decides to steal it so he can give it to a girlfriend or something," he said and walked away.

CHAPTER THIRTEEN

Thanksgiving, Jackie thought, was the most American of all the holidays. Christmas was universal. Fourth of July was picnics, parades and fireworks, but every nation had picnics, parades, and fireworks to celebrate some national event. Thanksgiving was church, football and turkey dinner with the family. Not many places had church on Thanksgiving anymore, but football and turkey on Thanksgiving; that was America.

He had not suggested church and football but had provided the turkey in what had been one of the most interesting and pleasant Thanksgivings she could remember. He had called her about nine Thanksgiving morning and told her he would be by her apartment about eleven thirty to take her to Thanksgiving dinner.

"Dress casually," he said. "Do you have a bathing suit?"

"A bathing suit?" she said perplexed. She was not used to wearing swimsuits to dinner. "Yes, I brought one, but where are we going?"

"I thought I'd take you to the beach for Thanksgiving dinner."

"I thought you had to go to dinner with all the other pastors."

"I just won't show up. It will just be another crowded restaurant. Nobody will even miss me. They may gossip about me, but they won't miss me. There are some very beautiful places left on this island and I thought you might like to see some of them. You have been here almost a month and haven't been out of Downtown, or Waikiki since you got here. But we can go to a restaurant if you like."

"No! No! Your idea sounds wonderful," she said not being entirely honest, but he had been such a help and friend that she did not want to deny him something he wanted to do.

She had never been one for picnics and camp-outs. That had been Cindy's thing. But he made it seem so simple and comfortable that she thought that maybe all previous picnics had not been handled correctly. They sat in beach chairs in the shade of the trees with the curve of the bay reaching in front of them to the sea. If she listened intently she could hear the waves breaking on the reef beyond the opening of the bay. Inside the bay all that was left of those waves was little wavelets lapped at their feet. He set the picnic basket between them as a table. They had Brie and crackers with their wine

98

while waiting for the coals to be ready on the small grill.

"Sitting here like this I can imagine what it was once like," he said. "Of course if we turn around and look the other direction we'll be able to see telephone poles, and street lights, and road signs, and all the scars that modern man can inflict on natural beauty."

"On the other hand," she said looking out over the water, "if it hadn't been for the scar of the road we wouldn't have been able to get here today, would we?"

"I might have known that someone from the most civilized, and sophisticated city in the country, would defend streetlights and telephone poles."

"You can have both, you know. San Francisco was probably a pretty place before the city was built but I doubt that Tony Bennett would have sung about leaving his heart among the trees of seven hills beside the bay."

He chuckled and said, "God, That's an old one. I didn't know anyone else remembered that song. We want both, don't we? When I first came to Hawaii there was what they called a "Hawaiian Village" in Ala Moana Park. No one actually lived in the village, but there were grass shacks and such with Hawaiians there to tell the tourist what village life was like. It was a picturesque and interesting addition. But I guess the city decided it was too expensive to maintain grass shacks."

He spread out the glowing coals, put the turkey thigh and the potatoes on the grill with the lid on and said, "Come on, let's got for a swim."

They swam and played; splashing and diving and it was amazing how in this beautiful and serene spot she could forget what it was that had brought her to Honolulu. When they came out he put the ears of corn, still in the husks, on the grill and they sat down again and finished off the last of the cheese and wine before they had their Thanksgiving dinner.

He had taken her out to dinner that evening, and then they had gone to see a movie. It had really been a very romantic day even though there had not been anything more physical than his holding her hand as they walked into the ocean. But that was yesterday and with the new day was the reality of why she was in Hawaii.

When she called to give Kunayoshi the license number of the car Susan had rented Jackie was told that he was gone for the weekend. She felt at loose ends. She thought she should be doing something, but she didn't know what there was she could do. Kimo and Marcella were both gone and she didn't feel comfortable calling Sloan and saying something stupid like, "I'm lonely, can you come and hold my hand for a while." She didn't feel like staying in the apartment so she drove down streets she had never been on before hoping to see a blue Camry with the license number of "BYN 575."

She stopped at Ward Warehouse for a cup of coffee, and then went and sat on a bench at Magic Island. When she got home about noon there was a message on the machine from Sloan, and it surprised her how good it made her feel to hear his voice. She called him back, and when she got through said, "I had a wonderful time yesterday, Doctor Sloan."

"Then why don't you start calling me Jim?"

"OK Jim, but as I was saying, I had such a wonderful time yesterday that I didn't even tell you about talking with Radford Lee Wednesday evening."

"When was that?"

"While church was going on."

"Learn anything?"

"I think so. When can you come over?"

"Well, I'm tied up this afternoon."

"Can you come for dinner?"

"Sure. I'll bring the wine."

He arrived about four-thirty and sat on the lanai talking to her as she began to prepare dinner. She told him about Radford and the locket. "Did it have a chain with it?" he asked.

"No. And I forgot to ask him about the chain. How did you know there was no chain with it?"

"Because I found a chain on the floor in my office and wondered where it had come from. It might have been with her clothing and fallen out when Radford and I were looking through her things."

"Mind if I go in and watch the news?" he asked heading for the bedroom.

"No. Go ahead."

"He sat down on the edge of the bed and turned on the set. The game show came to an end and after it four minutes of commercials which was included a promo for the local news, "Locally two cousins are charged in the death of two sisters - An inter-island barge company that has been operating between the islands for ninety years ceases operations - The city clamps down on the homeless in city parks - Those stories and more right after the national news."

He sat on the edge of the bed, his hands folded in front of him.

100

From time to time during commercials he got up and went out to see how she was doing and ask if he could help. She always said "No" and when the news would come on again would go back into the bedroom. The national news ended and in with all the commercials there was again the same promo as before. Finally there was the lead-into the local news and the Anchor said, "Two cousins were charged today in the death of night club dancer Cynthia Harcourt—"

"Hey, Jackie, get in here. It's about Cindy."

"For details on this bizarre story we go to District court and Joe Valenciano."

Jackie arrived in the bedroom wiping her hands just as Joe Valenciano came on. She sat down on the bed next to Sloan with the towel clutched between her hands.

"Yes, it is a bizarre story, Bill. When Cynthia Harcourt was found dead in the Nuuanu Hotel on the morning of October tenth of this year the police listed it as an accidental overdose. But a sister who claimed Cynthia Harcourt never used drugs came over from San Francisco to see if she could find who had given Cynthia the drugs that killed her. Today Manuel Rodriguez was charged with second-degree murder in the death of Cynthia Harcourt. Initially Rodriguez cousin, Reverend Douglas Bautista, was also charged in the case as an accessory after the fact. Source here say that those charges against him were dropped in exchange for testimony against his cousin.

"The bizarre thing is, Bill, that just after he had given testimony against his cousin, Reverend Douglas Bautista was arrested on suspicion of the murder of Susan Harcourt. Susan Harcourt was the woman that Reverend Bautista found dead on the steps of the First Aloha Christian Tabernacle three weeks ago. Sources here say that Susan Harcourt found out about Rodriguez and Bautista and that is the reason Bautista killed her.

"Both men are in police custody at this time. Rodriguez, as I said, is charged with murder in the death of Cynthia Harcourt and sources say that Reverend Bautista will be charged with first degree murder in the death of Susan Harcourt."

"Did they say anything about what lead them to arrest Reverend Bautista, Joe?"

"No, Bill, they didn't, but they seem to think they have enough evidence to get an indictment. There was hints that they may have a witness, but they haven't disclosed who that witness might be. There are even rumors that there is a third sister who was trying to find out how both the Harcourt women died. But again, Bill, that's a just rumor."

"Well, thank you, Joe, for filing that report."

She sat there crying with the towel crumpled in her hands. He turned off the television and got up, and went around the bed, and got a box of tissue, and gave it to her. She sat on the edge of the bed wiping her eyes. He left the room giving her some privacy. A little while later he heard her go into the bathroom, and when she came out the tears were gone and she was made up.

"I'm sorry," she said, and went back into the kitchen to continue preparing the meal.

He poured the wine while she put the food on the table. It was not until they had started to eat that she said, "You know that's not the end of it don't you?"

"What do you mean?" he asked.

"Don't you think it's a little strange that we make one phone call to Woodrow Haramoto and suddenly the police are hyperactive, and three days later they have charges against both Manny and Doug?"

"Well, if they had all the evidence all along and were just not acting on it then I guess it wouldn't take long to make an arrest."

"I don't know. Somehow I just have a feeling that Doug did not kill Susan. Everything is too pat with all the loose ends tied up."

"Intuition?" he asked.

"Maybe, but not entirely."

"Then if Doug didn't do it, who did?"

"I don't know. I have no doubts that Doug was involved with Manny in Jackie's death, but for some reason I'm just not comfortable with the sudden solution to everything. I just wish we knew who the witness is that the reporter said the police had. You don't think it is just the statement we gave them from Vanessa do you? I mean could the source have mentioned a witness, and the reporter thought that he was referring to Susan's death when he was really referring to Vanessa, and Cindy's death?" Jackie said.

"I don't know. But I will agree with you that something is not right here. Why in the world would Doug put the body on the church steps and then find it himself. As I said before, it would have been a lot smarter to dump the body in a sugar cane field somewhere. By the time they discovered it, it would have been so decomposed they wouldn't know who it was."

"Who makes appointments and keeps the records for everybody at the church?"

"Martha makes them for Pastor Bell, and Momi makes them for Doug. They both have certain times blocked off for call-in appointments. I keep mine. Someone wants to make an appointment with me the receptionist puts them through to me, and I make the appointment. If I'm not there, or in conference, they call back, or I call them back. I think Don, and Betty, and all the rest of them sort of do pretty much the same thing."

"What we have to do is look at the phone records, and the appointment books," she said with a puzzled frown on her face.

"What for?"

"I don't know, but we might find Doug did have some appointments with Susan, and if we do find that, then I will feel better that this things is closed. As you say, it is a little strange that Doug finds a body of a person he had killed. On the other hand, he may have done that just because he knew how people would think that he wouldn't do such a thing. Is he smart enough to do that?"

"Yes, he's devious enough for that. Today is Friday. Bjork has his Singles Fellowship tonight. That usually ends around ten, but people may be hanging around the church till eleven or so. We'll have to sneak in early in the morning. It seems we were doing this same kind of thing a couple of weeks ago to look at a computer. Now we have to check the phone log," he said shaking his head unbelievingly. "I'll pick you up about two."

"I'll be ready."

CHAPTER FOURTEEN

He parked the car half a block from the church so that the roving patrol that Doug had hired would not report that his car had been in the parking lot at two-thirty in the morning. They walked in the early morning coolness. Below them they could hear the hum of the cars of those headed home after spending the night on the town. Somewhere else there was the wail of a police siren. When he got to the corner he took her hand as he would have if he had been walking with Mary. It was an automatic gesture, left over from when he was married, and he almost withdrew his hand, but she took his in response.

They crossed the street and she held on to his hand as they walked up the steps to the front of the church, the steps where Susan's body had been found. The floodlights beamed upward along the white front of the church. Light glowed out from behind the twenty foot bronze cross attached to the wall making the cross look black by comparison. The lights were on in the foyer, but hardly seemed to be on at all compared the glaring white of the front of the church.

He wondered if there was anybody in the high-rises on the other side of the freeway watching them as they climbed the steps. They walked past the mango tree and up the second set of steps to the passageway to the offices. There was a lone, overhead light burning in the passageway casting shadows behind them and then to in front of them as they passed under it. The air in the passageway was still and hot. Through the windows could be seen one row of florescent lights on in the front office giving about one fourth the normal light. He let go of her hand to sort through his keys to find the one that would let them in. Inside he punched in the combination that turned off the alarm. There was a left over coolness from the air conditioning and the smell of pine from the Christmas tree that had been set up just that morning. The telephone log was sitting at the top of the receptionist neatly arranged desk. He took it and they went into his office. Away from the tree there was a musty smell that could not be identified as any one thing but was evidence that earlier there had been human activity.

They sat next to each other looking at each entry starting with the date that Susan had returned to the islands. You could tell when someone else had, for a while, filled in at the receptionist desk because the entries were not as neat as the receptionist's. They turned the pages one at a time studying the carbon-blue writing. Sloan had never realized before how many calls there were in one day. It started to get hot, and he went out and turned on the air conditioner.

They turned page after page, carefully checking all four entries on each page, and then Jackie jumped and said excitedly, "That's my telephone number, I mean Susan's, I mean Cindy's, I mean the number at the apartment." She paused for an instant, and then said, "That's the number of the apartment, and the name 'Susan Jamison'—Jamison was Susan's mother's maiden name. There it is, to Pastor Bjork. And the 'call back' box is checked."

He got up, and left his office, and returned a short time later with Don's appointment book. It was one of those weeks at a time spiral books and they opened it to the date of the phone log. They went through the names in his book from that day forward, but her name was not there.

"He sure uses a lot of whiteout," she said.

"Yeah. He whiteouts one name and puts another over it. That's when they change appointments," Sloan said, and held the book up to the light trying to read through the whiteout. "Well, there it is," he said finally. "The next day." He lowered the book. "At three in the afternoon. He whited it out, so she may have cancelled, or he may have whited it out after her death."

After that he started examining every entry that had been changed with whiteout holding the page to the light trying to make out the writing underneath. It was particularly hard because there was often writing over the whiteout, or on the other side of the page.

"Any more calls from her in the phone log?" He asked.

"I don't see any."

"Why do you think she used Jamison instead of Harcourt?"

"I don't know. Unless she already knew something and was being cautious."

"Here's something. Last line on a Monday, but we don't come in on Monday's. Monday's are our day off. And Don didn't have the duty that Monday. It's the Monday before Susan's body was found, and it is a whiteout." He held it up to the light, tilting the book a little one way, and the other, trying to read what had been written.

"I can't make anything out. It looks like F-O-O 18 Canning. Hand me that magnifying glass over there," he said.

They stood with their heads together peering through the

magnifying glass. They studied it for a long while, first one squinting at the magnifying glass, and then the other, and then she said, "That F is a seven. He makes the European seven with a cross on it. The one could be a J and the eight is an S. It's 7:00 JS Canning or Cannery. Is there a cannery in this town?"

"The old Dole Cannery. It's a shopping center now."

She sat down quickly, almost falling into the chair. "I'm scared," she said, "Let's get out of here."

They returned Don's appointment book and the telephone log to their places, and set the alarm and left. Fallen leaves from the mango tree snapped under their feet. A "skateboard" scurried away from a fallen mango and she jumped grabbing hold of him. She hung on to him as they walked to the car and he put an arm around her protectively, and he could feel her shaking.

"I felt like someone was watching us," she said after they were in the car. "Like someone knew we were there."

They pulled away and He said, "Would you like to stay at my place tonight. You might feel a little safer. I'm not hitting on you, after all, I'm twenty years older than you are, old enough to be your father, but if you'd feel safer you're certainly welcome. We—I have two bedrooms. And if you are afraid that someone is coming after you, they'd never think of looking for you there."

"Thank you. I don't feel like being alone tonight."

They were quiet driving to his place. They walked through the parking garage to the elevator, and after the dimness of all the places they had been the inside of the elevator was suddenly glaringly bright. They stood next to each other facing the door as they started to rise.

"What floor do you live on?" she asked.

"Sixteenth."

She remembered what Radford had said about a 'tall pastor'. That description would not fit Doug, but it would fit Don Bjork, and according to his book he had an appointment with Susan the evening before she was found. Did Radford know about that? 'Tall' would certainly have described Don Bjork, but it would also have described Pastor Bell, or Betty Clipper, or Doctor Sloan. She realized suddenly that Sloan had been controlling her investigation ever since that first time they had met in the park. He had told her what was going on in everyone's office, and life, except his own. They had invaded Doug's computer, and examined Don's appointment book, but she had never looked into any of Sloan's files, or examined his appointment book.

"One wouldn't live if they were to fall from that height, would they?" she said frightened, and testing him.

"Not very likely," he said.

They didn't say anything more the rest of the way up. When the elevator arrived at the floor he stepped out, and held his hand at the edge of the door holding it open for her. She hesitated, and he said, "Would you rather go back to your apartment?"

"No," she said forcing herself to smile a little to hide her fear. They walked along the outside walkway toward his apartment. It was just a wrought iron rail about waist high. Sixteen floors below them was the building's driveway. Across the driveway the building's landscaping gave way to the lush foliage-covered side of the hill that cradled Punchbowl Cemetery. It would be so easy for him to just grab her and throw her over the side. She set the thoughts aside and then felt a great sense of relief when he stopped in front of a door and took the keys out of his pocket.

He held the door for her to go in head of him. At the end of a short hall he pointed to one door and said, "That's the guest room. I don't know how long it's been since the sheets were changed, but they are clean. The door has a lock on it. And the bathroom is right over there."

She smiled, and relaxed a little, and said, "Thank you."

"Would you like a cup of coffee, or anything?"

"Do you have any herb tea?"

"Well, yes, we may have something around here." He dug through a shelf and said, "We have Peppermint, Apple and Spice, Orange Pekoe and Chamomile. Which do you want?"

"Chamomile would be nice," she said and sat down on the couch while he went in the kitchen and put the Pyrex measuring pitcher filled with water into the microwave. She looked around the room. It was not the kind of room she would have expected, and yet it seemed right. Across from her there was a wingback chair on either side of a pine armoire. There were speakers behind each of the chairs so she assumed that the armoire housed the record player, and the TV set. There was a brass floor lamp with a dark green shade next to each of the wingback chairs. The couch she sat in was large with a table at each end, and the coffee table in front of it. The early American furniture was too large for the room and was crowded even more by a dining room table pushed up against the kitchen counter with its spindle-back chairs pushed all the way in. The walls were covered with sketches and paintings. He came out a short time later with a cup of tea for her and a cup of instant coffee for himself. He sat down next to her setting the cups on the coffee table.

"Did Susan say anything at all to you about meeting with Don?"

"No, but then she wouldn't have."

"Why is that?"

"Of the three of us she is the only one that was religious. She had a great deal of respect for the church, and trusted all clergymen of any persuasion. Cindy and I used to tease her terribly about it. I mean, really riding her about believing that stuff. Whenever anything was on the news about any minister getting in trouble, like all of the stuff about the priest and boys, we would really rub it in, so she would not have told me if she was going to see a minister about anything."

"Do you feel better now?"

"Yes. I got really frightened there thinking he had seen Susan the same night she was killed. Do you think he could have done it? I mean the police said Susan died about one in the morning. Wouldn't Bjork's wife wonder where he had been?"

"He's also a police chaplain so he sometime gets called out at night. It wouldn't be unusual for him to be out at all hours of the night. If there's a bad accident for example, and they can't find out who the accident victim's minister or priest is, they'll call one of the chaplains."

"This thing gets more frightening all the time."

"You're all right now though, aren't you," he said looking concerned.

"Oh, My God," she said raising her hand to her mouth, and eyes filled with shock and fear.

"What is it?"

"Remember that Kunayoshi said it was Bjork that told him about Susan's letter to me. At the time we thought Kunayoshi was mixed up. I'll bet it was Bjork that sent me the letter and put it in Doug's computer. Bjork told me that he does most of the counseling in the church."

"But wouldn't Doug find the letter in his computer?"

"Not necessarily. Doug would file it in the letters folder using some strange combination of letter to identify it. Remember how Helen Abbot's memo was identified as ABBHEL? I figured out that Doug identified them with the first three letter of the last and first name. So ABBHEL stand for Helen Abbot. Bjork could have put any kind of combination of letters and unless Doug was looking through the folder to bring up another file, and happened to see what Bjork put in there, and was curious, and opened it, he would never know it was there."

"Does put a different slant on things. It's looking more and more like Bjork is our man, but why. What is the motive? Doug has to cover up his involvement with Cindy, but what's Bjork's connection to all of it."

"That's what we have to find out," she said with a determined and confident tone to her voice. "We'll get on it first thing tomorrow."

"You OK?"

"Yes, I'm fine. I think I'll go to bed now. Thank you, Jim, for everything."

* * *

Jacqueline Marqueoff woke up slowly, but even in that slowness of waking she knew from the very beginning that she was in an unfamiliar place. Everything had been unfamiliar recently. Hawaii was unfamiliar. Cindy's apartment was just beginning to be familiar, but she wasn't in Cindy's apartment. Cindy's apartment was noisy with sounds of passing cars and people walking along the sidewalk with boom boxes blaring. Sometimes at night there was the shouting of people in other apartments fighting. Those sounds came through the opened doors and windows. But there hadn't been any of those sounds during the night. It had been uncommonly quiet. In her half wakefulness she wondered where she was. Then she remembered the events of the night before and that she was in Sloan's apartment. When she had arrived in the early hours of the morning she had not realized the place was air-conditioned because at that time of night it was as cool outside as inside the air-conditioned apartment. The reason she had slept so well was that the closed windows kept out the noise and the air conditioner made sleeping with the light blanket comfortable.

She opened her eyes slowly. The room had been intruded upon by the light of day trying to make its way through the closed drapes. The drapes were a tan color and the light that got through made the room look as though it had been washed in a light-brown, mud color. She rolled over and the light-blue, digital numbers on the clock on the nightstand told her it was 9:17.

She sat up wishing the bathroom were attached to the bedroom so she wouldn't have to put something on to get there. She put on her dress, and opened the door cautiously in case he was still there. She didn't want him to see her without make-up. From the door way she could see a note propped up on the table next to the kitchen counter. She picked it up and took it with her into the bathroom.

She sat down on the toilet and started to read.

I've gone to the office to do a few things. I thought you might want complete privacy when you first got up. There is fresh coffee in the air-pot, at least it was fresh at seven. Should be all right.

On, and in, the vanity table in my bedroom are most of my wife's cosmetics that I haven't yet been able to bring myself to throw out. Some of them have never been opened. She could never step out, even to take the garbage to the chute, unless she was completely made up.

Open and use any of the new stuff you want. I don't know if this offer is an insult, or not, but the intention was good. Call me at the office when you want a ride to your place.

She smiled a little to think that he would offer her new cosmetics but had failed to put out clean towels. A moment later she saw them on a rack at the other end of the room, a complete set of obviously clean towels, and on the counter a tooth brush still sealed in its box, and next to it a small tube of toothpaste also sealed in its box.

She came out of the bathroom, and went to the kitchen for a cup of coffee and taking the coffee with her started looking around the apartment. The living room looked just a little bit less crowded in the daylight. His room was right next to hers with its door between the door to her room and the bathroom door. The bed was made. It had a headboard of dark wood that was ornately carved and reached almost to the ceiling. There was a small end table on each side of the bed. She saw the vanity he had mentioned in his note. There wasn't room for much else in the room and she thought that his room was probably smaller than the guest room.

Across the hall from the two bedrooms was another room that, like hers, also had the drapes pulled. In a corner by the drapes was a desk, a typewriter stand with a typewriter and a chair. The rest of the room had a plastic spread over the floor with an easel in the middle of the room. Paintings and sketches lined the walls and were stacked on the floor. There were stacks of empty canvasses on the floor in the closet. The closet door was open because it couldn't be closed with the canvasses reaching out into the room. She looked at the paintings and then went into the living room and looked at those that were hanging on the walls in there.

She went into the kitchen and got herself another cup of coffee. She walked across the living room and pulled back the drapes. Outside the sky was the color of sharks. She slid back the sliding glass door and stepped out on to the lanai. It was hot and humid and she could hear the muted roar of the freeway half a mile away. Every once in a while there was the sound of thunder. It sounded like a lots of sharks snapping at their prey.

She went and leaned on the rail with her coffee cup in her hand. The lanai ran the full length of the three rooms, the living room and the two bedrooms. It was a wall of solid glass, each room with a sliding door out to the lanai. She was on the top floor of the building, and with the view she had she wondered why all the drapes were pulled since it was not a question of someone seeing in and then guessed it must be because they were facing West and the afternoon sun would have burned in bright and hot. She looked down. Below her were the symmetrical lines of lanai rail after lanai rail until the symmetry came to an abrupt end against the blobs of color that were the tops of cars on the top floor of the building's parking ramp. For an instant she had an urge to tip her cup just a little and let a few drops of the amber liquid fall to the roofs of the cars below.

There were no buildings to obstruct her view. The low-rise and high-rise condominiums stepped down the side of the hill in front of her, but none were high enough to get in her way. Down by the freeway she could see the back of the church where Bautista had found Susan. She wondered if Sloan had walked to work, or taken his car. In the distance she could see the airport, and beyond that the low mountains of the Waianai Range. She took the last swallow of her cup and went back inside.

She took off her dress feeling free to walk around the apartment without anything on. If Sloan should return she would hear his keys in the lock before he got in. She rinsed out her under things and threw them in the dryer while she took a shower. The dryer had turned off by the time she finished her shower and make up. She took her bra and panties and hung them over the back of a chair to cool and dry completely while she got herself another cup of coffee.

She sat at the table and thought that nudity was a family trait. She liked to be perfectly dressed for the occasion, or totally naked. Cynthia enjoyed nude dancing. When they were girls the three of them might walk around the house all day without a stitch on. At home Jacqueline would very often sit nude at her computer trading on the stock exchange. She often wondered what those on the other end who were buying, or selling, would think if they knew that the person they were dealing with was at the very moment they were transacting business not wearing a thing.

As they got older Susan had become more and more demure until she got to the place where she would not even let the sisters with whom she had grown up see her wearing less than a modest bathrobe. They had teased Susan about that too and Jackie thought of how shocked Susan would have been at the idea of lying on the church steps with no clothes on. It was ironic that the most modest of the three of them, should in her death, be seen naked by hundreds of people.

It was eleven when she called Sloan and told him she was ready to leave. She met him at the elevator of level B of the parking garage. The first thing he said when she got in the car was, "Shall we go and see if we can find Susan's car, or do you want to go and get something to eat first?"

"No, let's go see is we can find the car" she said nodding, and she was glad that he hadn't asked all those normal questions most hosts asked of: "Did you sleep all right? Find everything you needed all right?" They were stupid questions that could only be answered one way and no matter what was answered it couldn't make the sleep of the past night any different, better or worse.

"I tried calling Kunayoshi this morning, but I was told that he would not be back in the office until Monday. I understand that it is the weekend, but I also think he doesn't want to talk to us. We will just have to go and see what we can find on our own."

They rode silently down Ward Avenue. "I looked around your apartment this morning. I see you're a painter."

"After my wife died I had to do something, and the church activities just didn't hack it. I started taking lessons at the Academy of Art and discovered that I really like it," he said, and they were quiet again as they headed along Nimitz highway to the Dole Cannery.

The tour buses were arriving in a steady stream dropping their tourists at the front door and then filling up the street level of the parking lot. It wasn't the height of the crowd yet, but there were four rental cars pulling their parking tickets out of the machine ahead of them. They started up the parking levels eyeing the cars on each side as they went up. They went all the way to the top. The fourth and fifth levels were completely empty. They went all the way down and were able to get out without paying because they had been in the parking ramp less than ten minutes.

He was about to pull out into the street when he said, "The cars been towed. They are not going to let a car sit in their ramp for three weeks."

There were no cars behind him waiting to check out and he backed up to the booth. "Do you know who has the contract for towing away cars from here?" he asked the attendant.

"Acme Towing," she said looking up from romance she was reading.

"Do you by any chance know where they take the cars they tow?"

"Sand Island somewhere I think. Don't know for sure."

"Thank you," he said and pulled out into the street.

They found Acme Towing and Storage beyond the container yard on Sand Island. A fat haole with graying hair and grease stained coveralls looked up tiredly from behind the desk when they walked in.

"We're looking for a blue Camry, license number BYN 575," Sloan said.

The man turned and looked through a large roller file without saying anything. He found the card, and pulled it, and turned to a calculator. "Seventy-two dollars towing. Twenty-two days at thirty-one dollars a day storage with tax comes to seven hundred eighty-four dollars and ninety-one cents," were the first words the man said to them.

Sloan leaned over the desk, resting his hands on the edge of it. "Well, before I pay that kind of money I want to see the car. Make sure you didn't put any dents of scratches in it, or steal anything from inside."

"It's one lane over down at the far end," he said. "Don't try to take it, it has blocks on the wheel."

It was not far away. "There it is," he said point. "Don't touch it just in case Kunayoshi's boys have the good sense to dust it for finger prints." They walked around it looking through the windows and Sloan said, "See anything?"

"No. Not a thing. That's weird. You don't have a car for over a month and not leave something in it, a sweater, a box of tissue, something," she said.

"That's just what I was thinking. The only thing I see is the parking ticket." It was on the dash. He turned his head to read it

113

through the windshield. "Can't read the date on it, but the time is 20:37. That's eight thirty in the evening. The ticket is still in the car which means she did not expect to do any shopping, or she would have taken the ticket with her to get it validated."

"What do we do now?" she asked.

"I don't know. But why don't we just go by and see if by any chance Kunayoshi is in his office."

They walked back and started getting in his car and the man stepped out of the office. "You gonna take it, or what?" he asked.

"No, but the police will be here pretty soon. They will probably take it."

The weekend receptionist on the detective's floor told them that Kunayoshi was not in, but Sloan saw him go into his office, and Sloan reached over to release the latch on the swinging gate and went through.

"Hey, you can't go in there," the woman called after them. Two uniformed officers got up from the desks where they were sitting and started down the hall after them. They caught up with them just as they got to Kunayoshi's office. An officer took each of them by the arm from behind and started pulling them out of Kunayoshi's office.

"It's all right, Men," Kunayoshi said and the officers let go of them.

Kunayoshi leaned back in his chair with his right elbow resting on the arm of his chair. It was a posture that just didn't look right on Kunayoshi. His right thumb was pressed against his jaw below the ear, and with his index finger he stroked the ridge of his nose running his finger from the bridge of his glasses till it dropped off the end of his nose.

He took a deep sigh and still stroking his nose said, "What is it this time. Have you come to tell me how to do my job or have you brought me some unimportant bit of evidence you think we haven't found yet?"

"We found the car my sister rented—"

"So did we," Kunayoshi said interrupting. "It is at the Acme Towing yard. My men are there right now."

"How did you find it?" Jackie asked startled.

"Our witness said it was on the Mauka side of the third floor of the Dole Cannery Parking Ramp. He saw Reverend Bautista meet Ms. Harcourt there."

"But it wasn't Bautista that met my sister there—" she blurted and out and then caught herself.

114

"If it wasn't Reverend Bautista, Ms. Marqueoff, who was it?" He stopped stroking his nose, and leaned forward putting both hands on his knees taking his usual frog position. He peered up through his glasses, his eyes bulging through the magnification of his glasses.

"I don't know. I just couldn't believe it was him. You don't expect ministers to do something like that."

"Isn't it a little late for a witness to be coming forward. Shouldn't they have come forward much earlier?" Sloan asked.

"Oh, they did. We just don't tell everything we know."

"You just said that your men were at the car right now. If you learned about earlier why are they there now or did someone just now tell you about the car?" Sloan asked accusingly.

Jackie kicked him in the leg and said, "I guess we just should have left it all up to you to handle," she said looking very contrite.

"I understand, Ms. Marqueoff," he said leaning back again and was suddenly very courteous. "You and I did not get off to a good start. I will admit that I don't like women butting into my business. Actually I don't like anyone, even my boss, telling me how to do my job. But I am trying to understand how you feel. I am married, and have children, and brothers, and sisters, and if I had lost two of them the way you have lost your sisters, I'm sure I would be acting exactly the same way.

"But we have the men who committed the crimes now, so pretty soon it will all be taken care of. We have a witness who saw her get into his car. We have found strands of her hair in Bautista's car. A scarf. We have a notebook with her writing in it and her fingerprints on it. And Bautista doesn't have an alibi for his actions that night. He claims he was home all night."

"What about his wife and children?" Sloan asked.

"She's off in St. Louis with the kids."

"Oh, that's right," Sloan said. "She takes them there every year about this time for Thanksgiving, or anniversary, or something."

"Now I really shouldn't have told you all of that, Ms. Marqueoff, but I wanted you to know that the men who committed the crimes against your sisters are both in our custody and the law will deal with them."

"Thank you, Mr. Kunayoshi, I appreciate your telling me these things. Can you also tell me the name of your witness?"

He smiled. "No. I can't do that; if for no other reason for that person's own protection. Not that you would do anything, but Bautista has lots of relatives."

115

"I understand. I just wanted to thank him."

"When the witness testifies before the grand jury everyone will know who the witness is and you can thank them then."

"Well, thank you, Mr. Kunayoshi," she said standing up and putting out her hand. He stood up and shook hands with her and they left.

Outside the shark colored sky had started a raining frenzy. They walked under the protection of the building to the point closest to the car and then Sloan ran to get it. By the time he got inside he was soaked. He pulled around as close as he could and she ran as best she could in her high heels, and jumped in on her side.

"Now what are we going to do?" she said as she wiped herself with tissue after tissue trying to get dry. "I couldn't just tell him about Bjork. I'll bet you dollars to donut holes that his witness is Bjork."

"And I'll bet you that Kunayoshi just heard about it. When somebody knew we had found the car, they told Kunayoshi about it which means that we are being followed, or at least someone knows what we are doing."

"I'm scared, Jim."

"Welcome to the club."

They were silent for a while head back toward his place and then he said, "Kunayoshi has everything tied up with nice little ribbons and he doesn't want anything disrupting his neat little package. Everything in it place to convict Doug. That explains why we didn't see anything in her car. Notice he did not say they found her fingerprints on, or in Doug's car, but on a notebook that was in Doug's car. The hair, the scarf, the notebook were all planted.

"Sometime after Susan was killed all those things were planted in Doug's car. I don't really like Doug, but I don't want him taking the rap for something he didn't do. I do kind of like Don, even if he is a little pushy, but I don't want him getting away with something like this if he did it. My question is why would he have done it? Doug had all the motive in the world. If Susan had found out about Cindy then he would have to keep her quiet. I can't really see him killing her, but then I can't see anyone killing another person. But at least Doug had a motive."

CHAPTER FIFTEEN

It doesn't rain a whole lot in Honolulu and Waikiki. There will occasionally be a little drizzle with the sun still shining which the Tourist Bureau likes to refer to as liquid sunshine. That is one of the reasons why it is such a good tourist area. The other side of the island is different. They frequently have rain which is why it is so green there. But every once in a while what started out as a hurricane out of Mexico will wear itself out over the Hawaiian Islands and it will rain everywhere. It rained for three days, and newscasters were sympathetic with the tourist and the locals alike, all of whom had their weekend ruined by the rain.

Pastor Bell did not preach on Sunday. He contacted the other pastors Saturday evening asking them to preach and explaining that he had a terrible case of the flue, congestion, stuffed head, sneezing, aching body and diarrhea. It was such a bad case of the flue that neither he nor Mrs. Bell were in church on Sunday. Doctor Sloan preached at the eleven o'clock service and Jackie attended just because he was preaching. As Jim explained to Jackie over lunch, having Doug in jail was just more than Pastor Bell could face.

"He's very hurt and embarrassed by this," Sloan explained. "Bell is very concerned about appearances and this does not look good. He can't face the congregation yet. He may not believe that Doug is guilty, but he won't be able to face the congregation knowing some of them may be thinking and wondering about it."

Sloan and Jackie spent most of Sunday afternoon, and Monday, on Jim's lanai wondering, and speculating, and wishing there were something they could do. "Did you notice how Kunayoshi tried to conceal the sex of their witness. I tried to catch him when I said I wanted to thank him, but he didn't fall for it. Do you think it could be Betty Clipper?"

"I don't know. She certainly has reason to dislike Doug. He is devastatingly blunt about her weight, and even worse about how she will never get married, or have children which really hurts her."

"Why does Bell let him get away with things like that? That is harassment."

"She can't tell Bell. Doug is Bell's fair haired boy, actually dark haired boy, Bell's protégée. Bell lost a son several years ago. I think

117

the son was five, or six when he died. Doug is about the same age as that son would have been if he had lived. Pastor Bell views Doug as the son he didn't have, the son who died, the son who would follow in his footsteps. Betty can't tell Pastor Bell about Doug for fear first of all that Pastor Bell won't believe her, which is probably true, and secondly that Bell will stop liking her for saying something like that about his beloved Dougie-boy."

"But what about Betty Clipper, do you think she could be Kunayoshi's witness?"

"Well, I think she is big, and strong enough to have done it, but I don't think she's the one. For one thing, she doesn't have a car. She would have had to check out one of the church cars in order to follow Doug around, which I don't think she did. Besides she would rather cry and have someone comfort her than actually do anything about a situation."

"Is there any way we can check on it?"

He looked at her inquisitively. "Well, yes. You have to sign the car out and back in when you use it. We have a couple old wrecks anyone on the staff can use."

They looked at each other for a moment and then he stood up saying, "I'll go check it right now."

He returned twenty minutes later and said, "Guess what. She did check one out on Monday, and returned it Tuesday morning. She put 'groceries' as her destination. So she did have a car out that night. But checking back through the log there were several Mondays when she checked out a car to get her groceries and kept it overnight."

"What about Radford. He described pretty accurately how it could be done. He was the one that mentioned a tall pastor. Do you think he's a witness?"

"He too has reason to hate Doug, but most of the time he just ignores Doug which makes Doug furious. Furthermore he has an alibi for that whole night. What we have to do is see if we can get Radford to tell us what he was talking about when he talked to you. We have to concentrate on Don. We know he had an appointment with her that night, or at least that she was in his book to meet him that night. We have to find a motive. Something that is so strong that Kunayoshi can't ignore it. As it is now Haramoto has gotten revenge for not getting the building contract and Kunayoshi has efficiently solved two murder cases which should look pretty good on his record."

* * *

At staff meeting on Tuesday everyone was very aware that Doug was not there. No one tried to sit in Doug's usual place and Pastor Bell sat at his desk looking worried and tired. The donuts and pastries were there as usual, and Damien and Betty helped themselves to several, as always, but out of deference to Pastor Bell there was a quiet that was not usually there when the staff was gathering for the meeting.

Pastor Bell asked Pastor Bjork to open the meeting with prayer and then he said, "I was able to get into see Doug yesterday."

"Oh, how is he?" Betty Clipper asked very solicitous.

"Well he is in as good spirits as can be expected—"

"Are we allowed to go see him?" she interrupted.

"Not really, but they let me in because he had asked to see me. Now we are all family here, and at this time we all have to pull together. The enemy is going to try and attack us with all kinds of lies, but if we stick by each other we will win. I am convinced that he did not do what they are accusing him of.

"Now the other thing he was involved in, but not in the way the media would like to tell it. His cousin Manny did call him saying that he had given this dancer—"

"Cynthia Harcourt," Sloan said interrupting.

"Yes, this Harcourt woman some drugs and that she had passed out. He asked Doug to come and help him carry her up to her room. Doug did that, and then stayed with the woman for a while after Manny left trying to minister to her, and praying for her. Doug says she was still alive when he left and I believe him. He may have been indiscreet but he did not commit a crime."

"Actually, Pastor Bell, he committed a crime when he didn't report it to the police," Bjork said.

"Yes, you're perfectly right, Don, but you know what I mean," Pastor Bell said running both hands nervously through his hair. "But I think we can understand not wanting to get a relative in trouble. It was a mistake. It was wrong. It was a crime, but I can understand how he felt."

"Yes, we certainly can," Bjork said, "but I just thought it best to let you know that it is not a good idea to say that he didn't commit a crime. At least not outside of this room. It's just a technical thing I know, but we don't want people to think you are condoning what Doug did." Bjork said spreading his hands.

"Yes. Yes. Of course. Thank you, Don. I want the rest of you to know that I talked with Pastor Bjork this morning and he has agreed to be acting administrative assistant until Doug gets back." He turned and looked gratefully at Bjork. "I really appreciate your filling in this way, Don."

"You're very welcome."

"Now we all have to stand by Doug. We have to do all we can to help him. He doesn't know who it is that the police say they have as a witness, but Doug says he thinks it might be someone from the church. Do any of you know anyone that might be telling the police these things?"

Everybody except Sloan seriously shook their heads, and Sloan said, "Huh, I can think of lots of people that might tell the police things about Doug. Some of them might not like Doug. Some might just not like this church. Some might just want some attention for a while. There's any number of people that might say things."

"Are you speaking generally, or do you actually know that someone from this church is that witness?" Bell asked.

"I have an idea of who it is," Sloan said.

"Who in heavens name?" Betty Clipper said pushing her bulk forward in her chair.

"Oh, I have no proof so it wouldn't be right for me to say who I think the witness is. That would be gossip, even slander. But I will tell you this, if I am right, the person that the police have as a witness against Doug is actually the one who poisoned Susan Harcourt, the girl Doug found on the steps a month ago."

"Oh, my goodness," Betty said putting her hands to her face and starting to shake with fear. "You mean he's still loose."

"He or she," Sloan said.

"She?" Betty asked sounding alarmed.

Sloan shrugged his shoulders and spread his hands, "Could be," he said.

The staff meeting broke up about eleven. Sloan called Jackie to tell her what had happened at the meeting and went looking for Radford to invite him to lunch and found him clipping the hedge at the front of the church.

"May I take you to lunch today, Radford," Sloan said. "There is something I want to talk to you about."

"You want to talk to me," Radford said looking perplexed unable to think of anything Doctor Sloan would want to talk to him about.

They sat at a table in the outside court of the restaurant. Radford had always like Sloan. As a young man who had to work hard to support a family and go to night school for his college education he had a certain awe of those who already had their degrees. Sloan always asked him what courses he was taking and how he was doing and had never looked down on him for being a custodian the way some of the people did. Most people who talked to Radford invited him into their office to do it, or stood leaning against a car in the parking lot. But Sloan took him out to lunch. Radford was curious, and a little apprehensive.

The outdoor court was almost deserted. It was still cloudy and most people were opting to eat indoors. In fact the host had to wipe the water off the seats before they could sit down.

The waitress brought their food and left and Sloan said, "Now, Radford, when you were talking to Miss Marqueoff you said your choice for the killer would be a pastor; a tall one. What did you mean by that?"

"I just said it. It would be easier for a tall person to unscrew the light bulbs, things like that. All the tall pastors are also big. They could carry a person easier than anyone else could. Besides, there's more tall pastors on the staff than short ones. Doug and Damien are the only short ones. I'm kind of short too, but I'm not a pastor."

"Did you have anyone one in mind?"

"Not really. I guess everyone thinks of someone they don't like who they would like to see be the one. But that's not serious."

"Do you think Doug did it?"

"No."

"Why not?"

"He will bully you with words and he will shout at you but inside he's unsure of himself. I think it would take a person that was pretty self-confident to do something like that. I mean something that's planned, not something you do because you got mad, and lost control. When you lose control you're not thinking. But to plan, and do something, you have to believe you can succeed. It takes a lot of self-confidence to believe you can kill someone and get away with it."

"You are a very perceptive young man, Radford," Sloan said admiringly. "I never thought of it quite that way, but yes it would require a great degree of self-confidence."

"In the staff meeting today Pastor Bell was saying that Doug thinks the witness against him is from the church. What do you think about that?"

"It's possible," Radford said. He had ordered the veal cutlet and had cut it all up in little pieces and was now mixing it all together with the rice and gravy, and volumes of ketchup he had pour on it.

"I told the rest of them at staff meeting that I thought that if that witness is in the church then the witness is also the very one that did it. What do you think of that idea?"

"That is also possible," Radford said taking the first bite of his mixed up concoction.

"Well, we are both agreed that Doug didn't do it, so who do you think did do it?"

"I'd rather not say."

"What about Betty? She's a pastor and she's tall," Sloan said testing.

"Naa," he said shaking his head. "She couldn't do it."

"Why not?"

"She's a crier not a doer."

"I agree. So who is left? Who do you think did it?"

"I would only be guessing."

"Radford, if Doug didn't do it, then the killer is loose, and I think he is the one that is the witness the police have. Now you, and I, have got to find out who it is because the police have stopped looking. We have to work together on this. I too have a strong suspect. I will tell you who my suspect is, and why, just as soon as you tell me who yours is, and why. I'm not trying to play a "you-go-first" game with you, but the reason I don't want to tell first is because I don't want to influence your thoughts and ideas. But we have to work together on this."

"OK. OK. My choice for killer of the month is Pastor Bjork."

"Oh, why?"

"I don't know exactly. But Pastor Doug, and Pastor Bjork had been at each other's throats for years. It used to be that Pastor Bjork wouldn't take any guff from Pastor Doug, but for the past year or so he has just curled up any time Doug said something. Once I heard them arguing and Pastor Bjork said that he would be glad when he was away from Doug at his new job. Pastor Doug said something about Pastor Bjork not getting that job because he was going to let those people know what Bjork did, or just what kind of a man Bjork was. Something like that."

"Maybe it was both, what he did, and what he was. You got any idea what Doug was talking about, what it was that Bjork did."

"No. They have never liked each other."

"You're right about that, but do you think Pastor Bjork hates Doug so much that he would commit perjury to frame him. Do you think he is capable of murder?"

"I think he is capable of anything to get his own way. Who do you think it is?"

"Don Bjork. For all the same reasons as you I guess. When He first got here he used to harass Doug all the time. In staff meeting he'd point out whenever Doug made a mistake and he always used to call him 'Shorty'. Doug is very sensitive about his height. You remember the Bjorks lived with us for a month when they first got here, before they got their own place, and you get to know a lot about a person when they live with you. Bjork likes to be in control and for the past year Pastor Doug has been in control. Bjork doesn't like that. When the Bjorks were guest in our house he tried to boss me, and my wife, around. He was never really rude, but he would always be making suggestions on how we should do things. I decided then that I was never again going to 'put-up' any more of Pastor Bell's staff, 'just until they find a place of their own'."

"So if Bjork is the one, Doctor Sloan, how are we going to catch him?"

"Just have to keep our eyes, and ears open, and be very careful."

* * *

She sat on the lanai looking out on the lights of downtown Honolulu and Pearl Harbor. She did not see herself as having moved in exactly, but most of her clothes were in the guest room closet. They had become good friends without the complications of sex. Aside from the fact that she had complete privacy, more or less depending on whether or not Kimo was at the door, Sloan's apartment was much more comfortable than the one next to Kimo. For one thing it was air conditioned, and it was a secure building. Anybody could walk up to her door in the other building. The only security she had there was that Kimo was between her apartment and the stairway. Here a person had to have a key or be buzzed in.

When she asked Sloan what he would do if Pastor Bell found out about it he said, "Well, Pastor Bell will probably tell me it doesn't look good, but then it doesn't look good to have one of his pastors in prison either. He may fire me, but then my leaving will only be sooner than later. I was planning to leave in the spring anyway. Actually I would welcome a reason to leave earlier."

Still they were discreet about their comings and goings and they were sure that no one knew about their 'living together'. She just felt more comfortable there. It was nice to be able to move around a room where everything in it did not remind her of either Cynthia or Susan.

He brought out the after dinner coffee and sat down at the table across from her, sitting sideways so he could easily look at the view of the city lights. "I think I've figured out why Bjork is our man. Radford gave me a clue when I had lunch with him today."

"I wondered what it was that you were preoccupied with all evening."

"I may just have concocted the whole thing, but I think Doug was blackmailing Bjork."

"Blackmail?"

"You remember when you discovered from Doug's files that Bjork had been having an affair and when the girl got pregnant he arranged for an abortion?"

"Yes."

"Doug was using that to get back at Bjork. Pastor Bell brought Bjork in from the Mainland. Bell had known him back there. Don used to ride and humiliate Doug all the time. Then a little over a year ago it stopped. At the time I couldn't understand the sudden change in Bjork. When we compare it with what we learned from Doug's computer that was about the time the girl had the abortion. With that information Doug started blackmailing Don, but not for money. Everybody knows Don has been offered this job in Seattle. He's supposed to leave this summer."

"Yes, he even told me about it."

"Well it is quite a boon for Bjork. From what I gather it is a rather prestigious job in certain circles. He will make enough to support his family, and still be able to work on his doctorate. Here he has to work as a pastor, have a second job as a police chaplain, and his wife teaches school just to make ends meet. As if he didn't have enough to do Pastor Bell announced this morning that Bjork would be acting Administrative Assistant until Doug got back."

"What does that mean?"

"It means that in a small way you can boss people around. If Bell is not going to be at a meeting of some kind he has his administrative assistant call everybody and tell them what they are supposed to do in his absence. Bell asked me if I would do it before he talked to Bjork, but I turned him down. I wouldn't touch that job with a ten foot pole."

"I'm glad you didn't take it. Doug could hold a grudge against you for just doing that."

"Now what Radford told me was that one time when he heard Bjork and Bautista arguing Don said something about being glad to be gone and Doug said Don would never get that job because Doug would tell them about him. Adultery and arranging for an abortion is not something any Catholic organization is going to overlook."

"How is that tied up with Cynthia and Susan?"

"This is where it becomes very speculative. Somehow Susan learned the truth about Manuel, Doug and Cynthia. She may have gone to the police and been ignored which is standard operating procedure for them. Not knowing what to do next she went to see Bjork. You said that she trusted clerics. If she respected and trusted them as much as you say she did, she probably did not think Doug had anything to do with Cynthia's death himself, but that he was keeping a secret. She might even have thought that, like a priest, Bjork could not tell anyone what he knew, and so she went to Him.

"Bjork saw his opportunity. In Cynthia's case Doug was only an accessory, and with his connections everywhere, and Bjork being a haole, and from the mainland, Doug would probably never even be charged. The police may have known everything about Cynthia's death all along, and were ignoring it, or rather sitting on it until Japco Construction got the church building contract. Bjork saw Susan as his way of eliminating Doug. The Catholics in Seattle were not likely to pay much attention to something someone in prison for murder might say.

"As I see it, Susan came to Bjork for advice. She was sure enough of him, trusted him enough, that she was willing to meet him at the Cannery. He took her to wherever it was that he was able to give her the poison and put her on the Church steps so that the investigation would center on the Church."

"But what about the letter to me? As you said, it had to have been mailed before he killed her."

"He sent that when he had his plans made. He got all the information from Susan. He didn't know if the police would really investigate it or not, but he knew that you would so he had to get you here. The letter didn't say anything specific, but he knew that after you got it you would eventually come. Even if he couldn't go through with the plan the letter would add to your confusion. The fact that you arrived on the day of her death was just coincidental. He put the letter in Doug's computer so that when the investigation started he could hint that if they looked there they would find out that Doug did know Susan and had even let her use his computer.

Remember, he is a police chaplain so he is known by all the officers. He has counseled them when they had marital problems, or problems with their children. He can drop hints all over the place if he wants to and has access to all kinds of things. My guess is that he got the poison from some policeman's wife who was threatening suicide sometime way-back-when, and just hung on to it, or he may have even gotten it from the evidence room. When we called Haramoto at Japco we actually helped Don in his little plan. With Doug in custody, or under suspicion, all Don had to do was give the police evidence. He may even have planted the poison container in Doug's office."

"What happened the weekend when I couldn't get a hold of her? I kept calling and calling."

"What he probably did was play on her fears and convinced her to go somewhere to be safe. He told her that since Doug knew what her address was, she would have to stay hidden."

"What are we going to do about it?"

"We can't go to Kunayoshi. First of all because he has pressure on him to see that Doug is crucified, and secondly because we don't really have anything. Aside from the entry in the telephone log we have no evidence except the entry in the date book, and that is only initials, which he can say he whited out when the party canceled their appointment. Our strongest evidence is the telephone log, and that's not very strong. As I said, everything I've told you is speculation. We may have to wait until the Grand Jury charges Doug, and then give everything we have, and our ideas to Doug's defense people."

"That's terrible. Isn't there anything we can do?"

"As I told Radford, Keep our eyes and our ears open, and be very, very careful."

"There must be something we can do."

"Well we could start checking with all the hotels and see if she was registered in any of them for those three days. But do you have any idea how many hotels there are in this city? There are over two hundred. And I don't think they are going to be very quick to tell you who may have stayed with them."

"Well the first thing I would do is ask Kunayoshi if he knows if Susan was registered in a hotel three days prior to her death."

"He'll never tell you."

She looked at him, the light from the living room shining on one side of her face. She was smiling slightly, but he could only see half the smile because the other side of her face was in darkness. He wondered if the other side of her face was frowning, hope on one side of her face, and fear on the other side, like the traditional theater symbol of comedy and tragedy, but she was only showing him the side she wanted him to see, the side with the smile of hope. "Maybe he will if I treat him very nicely and respectfully."

"How would he know if Susan stayed in a hotel?"

"I don't know, but whoever is telling him where Susan's car was may also have told him something about the three days prior to her death."

"Could be, I guess," he said skeptically.

"What else is there to do? Will you come with me? I'm scared to move around this town alone."

"Of course I'll come with you. But I think it would be better if you went into Kunayoshi alone. I'll drive you down there, and make sure you get in the building safely, but if the two of us show up again he'll be on the defensive. But if you are all alone, he will want to help a woman in distress."

"I see what you mean."

CHAPTER SIXTEEN

The Christmas tree on the detective's floor was one of the more interestingly decorated trees in the building. The theme in the Police Department for that year was THE SEA AROUND US. Many of the trees had been ecologically decorated with such ideas as saving the whale, or porpoises, or eroding beaches, but the detectives had gone with *Finding Nemo*. The tree had sand piled up in the form of dunes around the base of it with pieces of lava rock and derelict lifeboats. All of the characters from the movie were emerging from a mirror sea. Nemo and his father leaned toward them from their place on the deck of a small sailboat. The tree itself was completely decorated with multi-colored seashells and pink, black and white fan coral. At the top was the shell of a starfish.

She didn't know if it was the good will of the season, or that Kunayoshi was in a good mood because he had his case solved, but when she told the sergeant at the desk that she just wanted to thank Kunayoshi, and say good-bye, she was taken straight back to his office. He stood up when she entered, and reached across his desk to shake hands.

"So you're ready to leave, are you?" he said.

"Yes," she said sitting down in the chair he pointed to, "and I didn't want to leave without apologizing for the way I acted, and any trouble I may have caused you."

He was leaning forward with his arms on the desk, and he spread his hands as though he were about to catch a basketball and said, "No problem."

"And I want to thank you for what you did. It makes me feel a lot better knowing the one who did it has been apprehended."

"Just doing our job."

"Could I ask you one more question before I leave?" she asked very sweetly.

He slid back in his chair, his hands on his knees, his elbows in at his side taking the frog position, and looked at her suspiciously through his thick glasses but didn't say anything.

"Before I came over here I kept trying to call Susan but I got no answer. I called her for three days. I think I must have called her every hour." She managed to convey a desperate feeling of anxiety and worry. "Then when I got here I saw her picture on the evening news. What I was wondering is if anyone from a hotel had called to identify my sister, I mean cousin, after you showed that picture? I was thinking that maybe she was afraid Pastor Bautista was after her and had checking into a hotel. Could that have happened? Was she in a hotel? Or was she with him all that time? Kept prisoner by him, having all kinds of terrible things happening to her?" She started to cry silently, reaching for a handkerchief.

"Yes, she had checked into a hotel," he said leaning forward again. "That's why we didn't pay much attention to you when you and that Kimo Kahikokane came in here. She had registered under the name of Susan Jamison, and we had a fingerprint from the hotel registration card that matched your sisters. So when you came in here and said she was your sister and her name was Susan Harcourt I didn't believe you. I'm sorry about that."

"Jamison was her mother's maiden name, Mr. Kunayoshi. Can you tell me the hotel, and who it was that identified her?" she asked helplessly.

"No, I couldn't do that, Ms. Marqueoff. We may need her as witness."

"Please, Mr. Kunayoshi, please. All I want is to talk to someone who saw Susan before she died. Certainly my talking to her isn't going to make her testimony, or whatever less valid. You told me that you were married, and had children, and brothers, and sisters so I know you can understand how I feel. You have the killer now. My talking to this person isn't going to hurt anything. It would make me feel so much better just to be able to talk to someone who saw Susan just before she died."

He looked down at his hands for a moment and then looked up and said, "Her name is Toledo Torrez. She works at the desk at the Pacific Beach Hotel. But you didn't hear that from me."

"Oh, Thank you," Mr. Kunayoshi. "Thank you very much. I won't tell a soul," she said standing up. She shook hands with him and it was all she could do to keep from running down the narrow hall between the glass-fronted offices to get to the elevator that would take her down to the floor where Sloan was waiting for her.

"You say the Pacific Beach Hotel?" Sloan asked when she told him what she'd learned from Kunayoshi.

"That's what he said. Yes. Why?"

"It's probably just a coincidence," he said as they walked to the car, "but that is one of the hotels where we get special courtesy rates because we put our guest speakers there. The Pacific Beach more than any other because they give us the best rates, less than half the regular room rate."

"Then does the church pay for it?"

"Usually, but not always. When I've had visitors from the Mainland I've booked them in there, and claimed they were attending a conference, or something so they could get the courtesy rate."

"What are you going to do the rest of the day?"

"Start packing things up I guess."

"Are you talking about packing Cindy's and Susan's things?"

"Both. Have to close the place down."

"I have to get back to the office. I'll drop you off there but I want to be sure Kimo is there before I leave you alone."

He walked her to her door, Kimo calling a greeting as they walked by. Half an hour after he got to his office he got a call from Jackie, "I talked to Toledo Torrez and she gets off work at three. She said she'd meet us at the Beachwalk Coffee shop at three-thirty. Do you know where that is?"

"Yeah. I'll pick you up at three."

"OK See you then."

* * *

Toledo Torrez was waiting for them when they arrived. They sat down, and ordered some coffee, and Jackie said, "I really appreciate you meeting with us, Miss Torrez. As I told you on the phone Mr. Kunayoshi says you were the one on duty when my sister checked into the hotel."

"I wasn't the only one, but I was the one that handled her registration. I was on the evening shift that day."

"I know. The reason I wanted to talk to you was because I hadn't seen my sister in a long time, and I just wanted to talk to someone who had seen her just before—"

"I only saw her that one time. When she registered."

"I understand," Jackie said touching her eyes with a tissue. "Did she seem happy?"

"Yeah, I guess so. At least she didn't seem sad. Wasn't crying, or anything like that."

"Was anyone with her?"

"Yes. There was a man with her."

"Was it this man?" Sloan asked showing her a picture of Don that he had cut out of the church visitor's packet.

"Yes. That's him."

"Did they seem friendly to each other?" Jackie asked.

"Oh, yes. He seemed very concerned about her. I heard him saying things like she was not to worry about anything, and that he would call her the next day, and that everything would be all right."

"Did she seem worried, or anything that would make him say those things?"

"No, but she didn't say hardly anything at all. She signed the registration card, but he answered all the questions about the registration because it was a courtesy registration."

"Do you remember what that account was?"

"Sure. It was a church account. The same one where thy found her."

"Didn't he have to sign something too?" Sloan asked.

"Yes. There has to be an authorized signature from the company."

"So he signed the authorization."

"Yes, but it was a signature you couldn't read so I asked him how to spell it and I printed it above his signature. It was 'Reverend Douglas Bautista'. I remember, because he emphasized the 'Reverend' and because he was a haole and Bautista is a Filipino name. But you know, maybe his mother was real haole, and his father was just a little bit Filipino."

"Where was she when he was giving you that name?"

"Oh, she was over sitting down in one of the chairs. He told her to go and sit down while he took care of the bill and all."

"Did he go up to the room with her?"

"Yes. He and the bellman."

"Did you see her any other times, going in or out of the hotel?" Jackie asked.

"I don't think so. Not that I remember."

They talked a little longer and Jackie said, "I really appreciate your meeting with us, Miss Torrez. I'm sorry to have taken up your time like this, but I just wanted to talk to someone who had seen her right before she died. You helped me a lot when you said that she didn't seem unhappy or anything like that. Thank you. Thank you very much."

"Eez okay" She said as they stood up to leave.

Sloan and Jackie didn't say anything until they were out of the

131

parking ramp, and into the congestion of Waikiki's evening traffic.

"Well, what do we do now?" Jackie asked.

"It's too late to go to Kunayoshi with this now and I'm not sure he's the one to go to anyway. I don't think there is any doubt that we have enough to make Don look very suspicious, but let's sleep on it. We'll know better what to do in the morning. And rushing down to police headquarters now isn't going to get Doug released tonight so let's just wait till morning."

They were almost home when she said, "Do you think it is possible that the police don't know it was Bjork that signed her into the hotel?"

"I don't know. I've been thinking about that myself. If when Toledo called to identify Susan all they were interested in was who Susan was, and identifying her, they may have just asked for the registration card to get fingerprints so they could identify her. They may not have known that it was a courtesy registration. There are two separate cards: one for the guest, and one for the company, or in this case for the church, to fill out. Toledo may have been operating under the policy of answering only what they ask for, and if they didn't ask if there was a man with her, or if it was a courtesy registration, she didn't tell them."

"Or, on the other hand, Kunayoshi may know about Bjork, but now doesn't want to mess up his nice little package of solved crimes," Jackie said. "But if that's the case, why would he tell me about Toledo Torrez?"

"Or," Jim said, "he may know about Bjork, but doesn't have enough on him and hoped by telling you, Bjork would tip his hand. You know like Bjork tipping them about Susan car after we had discovered it."

"That bastards using me," she said indignantly

"Yes, he probably is. But I don't think there is anything more we can do about it today. I'll take you out to dinner and then I have to get to the final Christmas Program rehearsal. Betty's just tearing her hair about opening tomorrow. The choir isn't ready, her dress isn't ready, the decorations aren't ready et cetera, et cetera."

"How many performances are there?"

"Friday, Saturday and Sunday evening this weekend and Friday and Saturday next weekend. All the performances are sold out. But I'm sure I could find you a seat if you really wanted to go."

"Maybe I will."

* * *

It was almost ten o'clock before Sloan got home. Betty had worked on a couple of areas she considered a little rough and then they had gone through what was supposed to be the dress rehearsal. Sloan was the narrator and had to stay till the very end. After rehearsal Betty and he had locked the church and then gone to their offices to put their things away. By the time they left the church everyone else had left. He set the alarm and locked the offices. He walked her to the church car she had signed out. He kept telling her how good the choir sounded which was something she continually needed to hear.

Jacqueline was sitting in one of wingback chairs reading when he got home. She heard the keys in the door and was looking his direction when he entered. The light over her shoulder glowed golden through her light brown hair. She was wearing a light blue peignoir and nightgown, which contrasted nicely with the darker blue of the chair. She was, with her legs crossed, and her head turned looking toward him with the light shining through her hair, something he would like to paint if he had the ability.

"I just made some Chamomile tea," she said as he turned to lock and bolt the door behind him. "Would you like a cup?"

"Yes, that would be nice."

She floated up from the chair, setting the book on the lamp table as she did so, and he stood aside in the small hall way to let her pass through to the kitchen. Her peignoir floated behind her as though carrying the faint scent of her perfume with it.

He went and put his folder in on his desk and when he came out she was exiting the kitchen with a cup in each hand. "Shall we have it on the lanai?" she asked.

He went ahead of her to open the sliding glass door. He followed her out and sat down as she set the cups on the table, and then she went back inside and turned the living room lights off so they could sit in the darkness looking at the city lights. She came out closing the door behind her to keep the coolness of the air conditioning in.

Honolulu is like outdoor Christmas decorations. In the day time there is all the crudeness of the structures, but at night you don't see the buildings, just the lights. Towers and pinnacles of yellow or amber lights rising skyward on the outside stairways of high-rise apartments. At Christmas time it is even more of a glowing city with lights on lanais and on the tops of buildings. It was easy to pick out the buildings that have contests with prize for the best decorated lanai.

In the downtown direction could be seen strings of lights that circled every branch of trees from top to bottom. At the top of a thirty-six story new condominium going up was the construction crane with twelve golden reindeer pulling a red Santa in a red sled. Intersecting lines of blue lights at the airport outlined the runways. The freeway was a river of white light one direction and of red the other.

He breathed a sigh of relief. It had been a busy day and it was good to be home. There was something very pleasant about sitting there with her. They had gotten to the place where silences were no longer awkward. They were quiet for quite a while and then he asked, "So, how did the packing go?"

They had gotten so involved talking with Toledo and what she had told them that he had forgotten to ask her about it.

"It wasn't easy."

"No," he said. "Something like that is never easy. You are a very remarkable woman. I don't know that I could do it. As you know my wife's vanity is still set up in our bedroom and most of her clothes are still hanging in the closet. I think I am just now at the place where I can let the last of them go."

"It's always easier when you have to do something. When I saw all there was I realized there was no sense shipping all these things back to San Francisco. Marcella was there for a while and helped me. In the end we just bundled up most of the clothes and gave them to the Salvation Army. I kept the jewelry and other personal things."

"I'm sorry I couldn't help you today."

"Probably better that you weren't there. Marcella was exactly the right combination of understanding and pragmatism. She would ask me why I wanted to keep something, and when I thought about it, I didn't have a reason. You would probably have let me keep everything."

"Probably."

"Marcella went with me to see the landlord. He was very nice about everything. He agreed to take the furniture in exchange for this last month's rent and said he would return the deposit as soon as I was completely out. I think Kimo had something to do with that. He says he has someone who is ready to move in and needs a furnished place. I have a few more things I have to pick up tomorrow. I guess I'll be heading home as soon as we decide what we are going to do with what we know."

"I checked and Don is still using the same appointment book. I can't decide whether I should steal the whole book, or just rip out the page."

"You can't do that. Steal the book I mean. At least wait until the end of the year when he's through with the book. It's only a couple more weeks."

"I just hate the idea of that evidence getting away from us."

"Well, there's nothing we can do about it except testify that we saw it if we don't have the book itself. Anyway, as I was saying, I'll probably close up the apartment tomorrow and then I guess I'll move into a hotel for a couple of days."

"Why in the world would you do that?" He asked genuinely surprised. "You've been here for over a week now, why suddenly check into a hotel? You're welcome to stay here, you know."

"I know, but I don't want to impose on you."

"It's no imposition. I like having you here. You don't know how pleasant it was to come home and have someone offer me Chamomile tea, and I don't even particularly like Chamomile tea."

"Oh, I'm sorry, what kind do you like?"

"If it has to be herb tea, which at this time of night I suppose is the reasonable thing to drink, I guess my choice would be mint. But that's not the point. All I'm trying to say is I like having you here. You're a nice person to have around. I can get used to Chamomile tea. What I'm trying to say is that you are not at all imposing on me, in fact I like having you here."

"I don't want to give any of your church people anything to talk about. As long as I had the apartment I could say that was where I lived and was just visiting here."

"I told you before that I was planning to resign soon anyway and I don't care what they say," he answered.

"It's not you I was thinking of."

"Who then?"

"Pastor Bell."

"Pastor Bell?" he exploded totally surprised.

"My grandfather set up, and was president of a financial firm. He had an excellent reputation but after thirty years some of his brokers were charged, and later convicted, with fraud and insider trading. My grandfather knew nothing about it, but when this information came out there were rumors, and gossip, about things that had nothing to do with finances, or ethics. And the talk was never about my grandfather, just about the people around him, but clients left in droves. My grandfather was a good man. From what you say Pastor Bell is a kind, caring person. He is a good man, but I will bet people are even now wondering if they shouldn't leave the church. When the rumors really start flying I don't want them to also be able to say," she tilted her in a disdainfully superior way and said, "'Well, not only was one of his staff charged with murder, but that other one was living with a San Francisco woman. And you can't tell me Pastor Bell didn't know about it.' For my grandfather's sake, as well as Pastor Bell's, I don't want to give them anything to talk about."

"As I said, you are a remarkable woman. Do whatever you think is best, but just know that you are welcome here any time."

They were silent again for quite a while, both of them thinking they should be going to bed, but at the same time reluctant to leave the pleasantness of the evening and each other's company. Once she said, "Do you want another cup of tea?"

"No thank you," and they had both lapsed back into the pleasant silence.

Somewhere a phone rang. It was persistent and finally he looked around puzzled and said, "Is that our phone? At this time of night?"

He got up and opened the door and the sound of the phone filled the night. He went in and answered it. "When?"

She heard the concern in his voice, and stood up, and stood in the doorway to better hear what was said. On one side of her was the warmth of the evening, and on the other side the coolness of the air conditioning.

"Yes. I'll get right over there—Yes, I understand—Has Pastor Bell been told?—OK I'll see you there."

He came toward her hurrying for the lanai. "That was Don. He says there is a fire at the church." He pushed by her and went and stood at the rail looking toward the church. "Well, I don't see any flames yet, but there is smoke."

"I don't see anything," she said coming and standing next to him. He point over the rail and she said, "Oh, Yeah. How come Don called you?"

"The police called him, but he lives on the other side of the island, and I'm the one that lives closest to the church. I have to get over there," he said heading toward the door.

"Be careful," she said following him to the door as he went out. She shut the door behind him turning the bolt, and pushing the button in the doorknob to lock it.

* * *

The fire trucks and the police were already there when Sloan arrived. The police tried to stop him until he told them who he was. He left his car parked next to a squad car and they let him through to where he could talk to the fire captain. The fire was at the front of the church. From where they permitted him to stand he could see the flames leaping up from the benches of the choir loft, consuming the Christmas trees and decorations, and the wooden pulpit. He had just finished explaining to the fire chief that the choir robing room was under the choir loft when Pastor Bell joined them.

"That's probably where it started," the captain said.

Sloan stood looking at the fire trying to remember exactly what had happened when practice ended. He and Betty had checked the front door and then exited through the side door making sure it locked behind them. Then they had gone to their offices. He didn't remember if Betty had looked in the choir room or not. He knew that he hadn't. Had they left someone in the church when they closed up?

Pastor Bell just stood there shaking his head looking at his church burning. Sloan stood next to him and put an arm around his shoulder.

"How can it all happen at once, Jim?" Pastor Bell asked. "Doug in Jail. Scandal of one kind or another everywhere I turn, and now this. Is God testing me? Is God punishing me for something I did that I don't even remember?"

"I don't think God has to resort to setting a building on fire to teach us something. The things that have been happening in the church are all things done by some person, not by God," Sloan said, and as soon as he said it he was suddenly very much afraid. He looked at his watch trying to remember when it was he had answered the phone. Was that ten, or fifteen minutes ago? It didn't make any difference if Don had not been at home at all but had called from his cell phone. He could have called, and then waited and watched for Sloan to leave.

He left Bell standing by himself and found a police officer with yellow stripes on his arm. "Sergeant, can you send a couple of men with me? I think I know who started the fire and where he is."

* * *

Jackie stood at the lanai rail looking at the fire. As she stood watching she saw it change from just smoke and then to a glow against the smoke and then she saw the flames coming out of the roof. The pleasant evening of sitting on the lanai had come to an abrupt end with the phone call.

After closing the door behind Jim she turned on the light, and went back to the lanai to stand and watch. She left the Lanai door open so she could hear if the phone rang. She didn't know how long Jim had been gone, but it surprised her to hear his key in the door. It also surprised her to realize how concerned she had been about him. She stepped into the living room just as the front door swung open and Don Bjork came through the door.

"How the hell did you get in here," she asked stopping petrified in the middle of the room.

"With the key," he said smiling, and holding up a ring with three keys on it.

"Where did you get them?"

He approached her slowly, still smiling. "We stayed with the Sloans when we first got here. He gave me a set of keys and told me to have some more made. When we left I just didn't turn all the keys over to him. After all, I had paid to have them made."

"What are you doing here?"

"Taking care of loose ends. Incidentally, you look particularly attractive tonight. Sloan is very lucky to have someone as attractive as you living with him. But isn't he a little old for you?"

"I think you better leave," she said edging slowly toward her bedroom door. If she could get in there she could lock the door.

"But I have some loose ends to take care of. I told you that. You think I killed your sister, don't you?"

"What a preposterous idea. The police have charged Pastor Bautista with that. Why in the world would I think you had done it?"

He turned around and she thought for a moment he was leaving, but he only went as far as the hallway to turn off the kitchen lights, and then the living room lights.

"What are you doing?" She was terrified, but there was no terror in her voice, only a demand for an explanation as one might demand it from a child.

In the semi-darkness with only the light from outside coming through the plate glass doors to the lanai she could see that he had not moved from the hallway where the switches were. She slid her feet along the carpets gliding slowly toward her bedroom hoping he was not noticing her movement.

"Why, I'm turning the lights off. Can't you tell?"

He was playing with her, the cat with the mouse, and she had to play with him to put off as long as possible the end. The longer she could stall him, the better her chances were.

"Why are you turning off the lights?"

"So no one will see what caused you to fall from the lanai. Everyone will assume that you leaned over to far to see the fire."

"What in the world makes you think I'm going to fall from the lanai?"

"I'm going to see to it that you do," he said, and she realized that he was closer to her than he had been before.

She turned and bolted for the bedroom, but he was at the door, pressing against it before she could slam it shut. She ran to the sliding glass door leading to the lanai, but the drapes were drawn and she got tangled up in them before she could get the door open. The lamp next to the bed came on, and he came toward her. She turned, and ran over the top of the bed, having trouble keeping her balance on the bouncing bed, and found herself in the corner of the room hemmed in by two walls and the bed.

He was standing at the foot of the bed halfway between the door to the lanai, and the door to the living room. "This was our room when we were here. I know exactly where the light switches are, and how the door to the lanai opens. I know everything about this room."

"Why do you want to kill me?"

"Because you know too much?"

"What do I know?"

"You may not know it for a fact, but you think I killed your sister, and you are trying to prove it."

"Did you?"

"Since there is no one here but you and me, and since in just a few minutes you are not going to be able to talk ever again, I tell you. Yes, I killed your sister," He said smiling. He was enjoying tormenting her.

"You know, Pastor Bjork, when we first met you told me only a sick person would do those kind of things. Are you insane, Pastor Bjork?"

She hoped calling him pastor, and using the word insane would influence him some way.

He smiled and took a lumbering step toward her. "Who's to say who is sane or insane?"

"Why did you kill her? What did she ever do to you?"

"Nothing. But I needed her dead to frame that pompous ass Bautista."

"And why are you going to kill me? Do you need me dead too?"

"Only because you know too much."

"I didn't know anything till you told me just now. You blew it. You could have gotten away with it but you panicked and came after me, but you're not going to get away with it. Whatever made you think I knew something?"

"The moment you left my office after you first made an appointment to see me I had a police officer who owes me a big, big favor start following you. When he couldn't do it personally he had someone else do it. I know about your early meetings with Sloan at Magic Island, and about the nights the two of you went to the church in the wee hours of the morning. After the second time you came back here with him."

"So are you going to kill me just because I spent the night in a man's apartment?"

"No. Because the next morning the two of you drove directly out to the Cannery parking ramp looking for your sister's car. You did that before I had told Kunayoshi about it. Not much before, but enough before that I knew you were on to something. What did you find that let you know where the car was?"

She grabbed the lamp next to the bed and threw it at him, plunging the room into darkness, and ran for the door as he ducked instinctively to avoid the thrown lamp. She felt his hand on her shoulder as she went by, and then the peignoir sliding off her shoulders. She ran through the living room toward the lanai. If she could get there she could start screaming, but she felt him tackle her, pulling her to the floor, ripping her nightgown in the process. She scrambled along the floor screaming at the top of her voice hoping that someone would hear her, and at least complain to the police about all the noise.

She managed to get away from him and stood up, throwing over one of the wingback chairs in the process. He scrambled over it, and grabbed an ankle pulling her down. She kept crawling, headed for the open lanai door. She knew that's where he wanted her to be so that he could throw her over, but at the same time if she could get there ahead of him she might be able to slam it shut behind her and keep screaming till someone got there. But she didn't make it. He was right there, crawling along the floor behind her, and then he pounced and was on top of her. She tried to roll out from under him, but he had all his weight on top of her. His hands were all over her face trying to clamp a hand over her mouth to keep her quiet and also hitting her. She shook her head back and forth even as she was pinned to the floor.

He had something in his hand and was trying to hit her on the head with it. She kept screaming, and pounding him with her fists, and kicking, and rolling back and forth trying to get away from him. She felt a knee pin one elbow to the floor and then the lights suddenly went on. Lying on her back looking up she saw him above her looking toward the doorway, his mouth open, and his eyes wide with surprise. She saw Sloan rush in and run toward them. She felt the wind created by Sloan's foot passing just above her face as he kicked at Don. The toe of his shoe caught Don on the chin, and Don's head jerked back. She pushed Don off her, and scrambled to her feet. Sloan was right beside her. He yanked the tablecloth from off the table, sending the vase and candlesticks flying and wrapped it around her as he put his arms around her.

"He told me he did it, Jim. He told me he killed Susan. He was trying to kill me because he thought I knew. He was going to push me over the rail."

"I know. I know," he said as he gently guided her from the room. "It's all over now. Everything is all right." He guided her into her bedroom, and behind them they could hear one of the officers reading Chaplain Bjork his rights.

CHAPTER SEVENTEEN

They sat on the lanai looking at the lights of the city. It had been more than a week since Don had been arrested and charged. She was wearing the same suit she had worn when she arrived. It was sophisticated and traveled well. She had said her good-byes to Kimo and Marcella that morning and in the afternoon Sloan had been with her when the casket with Susan's body had been put on an earlier flight. Her bags were packed and waiting by the door. In front of them the beauty of the lights of Honolulu at night spread out with all the glittering sentiments of the Christmas season.

"Do you think they will want me to back to testify?"

"With his confession I don't think there will be any need for that. If for some reason his defense could get his confession thrown out then they might want to call you to testify about his confession to you and attempted murder."

"How did they ever get him to confess?"

"Well, to be honest with you, Inspector Wo and I tricked Bjork a little bit. Wo and Kunayoshi are both in line to be head of homicide and so they are very competitive. They both try to outdo the other. Consequently Wo was very cooperative and eager for any help I could give him. We told Bjork that I had both his office, and this apartment bugged. To prove it we played an old tape I had of him counseling someone in his office."

"You mean to tell me this place is bugged too? You have everything he said to me on tape?"

"Of course not. Why would I want to listen to what I say to myself? But we convinced Bjork that if I could bug his office and Doug's office I probably had this place bugged too. Wo convinced him we had a tape of everything the two of you said while he was in here."

"Didn't he want to hear it?"

"Of course, but Wo said he couldn't listen to it because it was evidence."

"You are a sneaky bastard, aren't you?"

"Yes. And aren't you glad."

"What's going to happen to Doug?"

"Right now we have a humble Doug, a contrite Doug, a repentant

Doug, an 'Oh please do forgive me' Doug. This morning Pastor Bell reminded us all of the scripture that says if a man is taken in a fault we who are spiritual should restore him. So he's back on the staff. He doesn't have the authority he had before. People will forgive, and some might even forget. It won't be long before he is his old arrogant self."

"And what about you, Doctor Sloan?"

"You still have trouble at times calling me Jim, don't you?"

"OK Jim, what about you?"

"I'll do just as I had always planned. After the first of the year I'll give Pastor Bell my letter of resignation, and put the condo on the market. The market is good right now. I should clear three hundred thousand or better. I'll probably put most of it in some mutual fund, and go rent a room on the North Shore, or maybe buy a cheap place in Montana, or Carolina where I can live comfortably on my earnings."

"When you sell the place why don't you let me handle your money? I could probably do better for you than any mutual fund can, and I would never charge any commissions."

"Maybe I'll take you up on it."

"I might even be able to make you a rich man. Not Vanderbilt rich, but very comfortable."

"I am no longer really concerned about being rich. With the sale of the condo, and other things I'll have enough. What I want now is tranquility. I want to do my painting, and play tennis, and go sailing whenever I want without worrying about what someone will think, or if I have enough money to do it. I think there are places where I can do that. If I were twenty years younger I would probably be interested in getting rich, but then there would be a lot of things I might be chasing after if I were twenty years younger, including you."

"Thank you, Jim Sloan. I take that as a very high compliment. I will be hurt if you do not stop by San Francisco to visit me on your way to wherever you're going."

They were silent for a moment and then she said, "Well, I have a little time left. May I make you a cup of Chamomile tea before I leave?"

"Oh, please. Don't ever offer me Chamomile tea again. I detest it."

"I know," she said chuckling.

They were silent until the phone sounded its double ring

indicating there was someone at the building door.

"That will be my taxi," she said standing up and heading inside, and he got up and followed her.

"Are you sure you won't let me take you to the airport?"

"No. I arrived in a cab, and I'll leave in a cab. I don't want any gateway good-byes, or a lei around my neck. So don't try to give me that lei that you have in the refrigerator."

He answered the phone telling the driver they would be right down, and then stood in front of her by the suitcases. She reached up and kissed him lightly on the cheek.

"Now if you come to San Francisco, I will meet you at the airport. You can bring me a lei if you want, and I will insist you stay with me instead of in a hotel."

She turned and walked out of his apartment, and he walked behind her with her suitcases. They rode down on the elevator, and he stood by awkwardly while the driver put the bags in the trunk. He held the door for her, and she got into the cab.

"We work well together, Sloan," she said leaning out of the cab window.

"That's true, but I don't want to get involved in anything like this ever again."

"I promise you that next time it will be better things we're involved in."

"I'm sure of it. I guess it would be crass under the circumstance to say Merry Christmas, Jacqueline Marqueoff, but I do wish you all the best."

She smiled. "I know you do, Doctor James Kelinworth Sloan. The coming year will be good for both of us."

She leaned back in the seat and the driver pulled away. He stood watching the taxi pull out into the street. He hoped to get one last look at her, but in the darkness inside the cab he could not see if she had turned to look back at him.

It had been raining earlier and the water on the black driveway reflected the red taillights of the departing taxi. The taxi turned into the street, and then it too was hidden from view by the embankments and shrubs. He stood there for a long time looking at the wet, empty street. It started to rain again, and he walked slowly toward the plate-glass, front doors not really caring that he was getting wet. Fifty-five was a lousy age to be, and Christmas was a lousy time of year.